CRYPTID CHRONICLES
THE CAVE

ETHAN HAYES

FREE REIGN
Media

CONTENTS

PREFACE

I've always been captivated by the mysteries of the unknown. Growing up, my summers were spent flipping through dusty books on cryptozoology and listening to my grandfather's hushed tales about encounters in the woods that no one dared speak of in daylight. Among all the legends—the Loch Ness Monster, the Chupacabra, Mothman—one always stood taller, both figuratively and literally: Bigfoot.

For me, Bigfoot isn't just a creature; it's a symbol of the vast, untamed wild that still holds secrets beyond our comprehension. It represents a question humanity has been asking since the dawn of time: What else is out there?

When I began writing these thrillers, I wasn't just spinning tales of suspense; I was weaving together pieces of wonder, fear, and the undeniable allure of the hunt for something greater than ourselves. Through the lens of fiction, I could explore the "what-ifs" that keep so many of us looking over our shoulders when the forest falls eerily silent.

But these stories aren't just about Bigfoot. They're about us—our desires, our obsessions, and the lengths we'll go to in order to uncover the truth. They're about the adventurers who risk everything for a chance to glimpse the extraordinary and the skeptics who find themselves questioning everything they thought they knew.

So, as you turn the pages of these novels, I invite you to step into the wilderness, to listen for the snap of a twig or the faint rustle of leaves behind you. These are stories born of curiosity and crafted with the hope that they'll ignite yours.

After all, the forest is vast, and the truth is still out there.

– Ethan Hayes

PROLOGUE

The cavern loomed before him, a black maw in the face of the mountain. John Hadley paused at the threshold, his breath clouding the cold night air. The beam of his headlamp sliced through the darkness, illuminating jagged stalactites like the teeth of a slumbering beast. He tightened his grip on the walking stick in his hand—a practical tool doubling as a steadying crutch for his stubborn legs—and took a deep breath. His chest protested, the dull ache a reminder of the pills he'd left untouched back at the cabin.

"It's just a precaution, Dad," Emily had pleaded with him, her voice tight with worry. "You're not exactly in peak health anymore. This... obsession is going to kill you."

Obsession. The word stung, but John knew better than to argue. He was a man driven by purpose, by the pursuit of truth. A lifetime of ridicule, academic scorn, and late-night radio interviews with conspiracy theorists had earned him a reputation: the cryptozoologist chasing shadows.

But this time, he wasn't chasing shadows.

This time, he was going to prove them all wrong.

The cavern system had been a revelation—a network of tunnels that snaked deep beneath the forest floor, untouched by human hands. A recent landslide had exposed the entrance, and within days, John was combing the area. Footprints, faint but unmistakable, had pressed into the damp earth near the mouth of the cave. They were enormous, far larger than any human's, and fresh.

"Emily," he had said over breakfast, a grin splitting his weathered face, "this is it. This is where it lives. I know it."

She had shaken her head, her frustration edged with something he didn't want to admit looked like fear. "Dad, I'm begging you. Stay out of those caves. You don't even know what's in there. And your heart—"

"My heart can handle it," he had snapped, more sharply than he'd intended. The silence that followed had been heavier than the storm clouds rolling in over the treetops.

Now, standing at the edge of the unknown, he felt a pang of guilt. He should have said something else, anything else. But he'd apologize when he got back. When he had proof.

The first few steps were easy enough. The ground sloped downward, the rocky floor uneven but manageable. The light of his headlamp bounced off damp walls, slick with condensation. The air grew colder, and the musty smell of earth filled his nostrils. He paused to listen. Above the drip of water somewhere deeper inside, there was… something else. A faint sound. A low hum, almost like breathing.

"Just the wind," he muttered to himself, though he gripped the stick tighter.

John pressed on, his pulse quickening—not from exertion, but from anticipation. The footprints had led him here. He could still see them in the faint dust of the cave floor, impossibly large, impossibly real. He felt a triumphant thrill rise in his chest.

This was it.

Suddenly, the light from his headlamp flickered. Once, twice, then darkness. He fumbled with it, smacking the casing against his palm. A faint glow returned, but weaker now. The beam barely penetrated the shadows.

And then he heard it.

A low, guttural growl.

The sound reverberated through the cavern, low and primal, vibrating in his chest. His breath hitched as he swung the dimming light in every direction. The beam caught glimpses of wet rock, a flicker of movement, and then—nothing.

"Who's there?" he asked, his voice echoing, trembling despite his resolve. It was a question that simply spilled from his mouth instinctually even though he knew what it was.

Silence.

John took a cautious step back, and his foot struck something soft. He looked down. The remains of some animal—a deer, its bones picked clean—lay scattered across the floor. The air now stank of decay, and something else: musk, heavy and animalistic.

He wasn't alone.

The growl came again, closer this time. His light flickered once more, and in the brief moment before it went out entirely, he saw them: two eyes, impossibly large and gleaming in the darkness, watching him.

The last thing John Hadley felt was his heart, hammering wildly in his chest, before it betrayed him completely.

CHAPTER 1

Emily Hadley twisted the coiled cord of the landline phone around her finger, the receiver pressed tightly to her ear. Her heart thudded in her chest as the call rang out, unanswered, for what felt like the hundredth time. She bit her lip, suppressing the rising tide of frustration and fear that threatened to overwhelm her.

"Come on, Dad," she whispered under her breath. "Pick up."

The call clicked over to the answering machine. His own voice, warm and slightly gravelly, echoed back at her:

"You've reached John Hadley. Leave a message, and I'll get back to you. Unless, of course, I'm out in the field. If so, you're just going to have to wait. Science waits for no one!"

The recording cut off with a beep, and Emily slammed the receiver back onto its cradle. She leaned against the kitchen counter, staring at the phone like it might suddenly spring to life and ring. The silence in the house felt oppressive.

It had been over 24 hours since she'd last seen him, standing at the front door with that damn walking stick in one hand and his beat-up satchel in the other. He'd been so confident, his blue eyes gleaming with the same determination that had driven him for decades.

"This is it, Em," he'd said, grinning. "The evidence I've been waiting for. Bob and I are going to find it this time, I know it. When we get back, they'll have to take me seriously. No more calling me a crackpot!"

Emily had stood in the kitchen doorway, arms crossed, her frustration bubbling just beneath the surface. "Dad, you've said that before. A hundred times. And you're not feeling well. What if something happens out there?"

"Bob'll be with me. Besides, it's just for the day," he'd said, waving off her concerns.

And then he was gone.

Now, the clock on the wall ticked loudly, marking every second since he'd walked out the door. She'd tried to convince herself he was fine, that the weather or some mechanical issue with Bob's truck had simply delayed them. But the longer the hours stretched on, the harder it became to push the dark thoughts from her mind.

Emily picked up the receiver again, dialing a familiar number. Bob's home.

It rang three times before a voice answered, raspy and a little impatient.

"Yeah, this is Bob," came the raspy voice on the other end of the line.

Emily gripped the phone tighter, her pulse racing. "Bob, it's Emily. Where's my dad? He said you were going with him yesterday, but he hasn't come back. I've been trying to call him all day."

There was a long pause. Too long.

"Emily," Bob finally said, his voice hesitant, "I haven't seen your dad in months."

Her heart skipped a beat. "What? No, that can't be right. He told me he was going with you yesterday—to some caves. He said you'd be with him."

Bob let out a heavy sigh. "Caves? Emily, I don't know what he told you, but I'm not involved in any of that. Your dad and I... well, we had a bit of a falling out. Haven't spoken to him since summer."

Emily leaned against the counter, her mind racing. "A falling out? What do you mean? He didn't say anything about that. All he said was that you'd be with him."

"Yeah, well, that doesn't surprise me," Bob said, his tone softer now. "Look, I wish I could help you, but I don't know anything about caves or where he went. If I did, I'd tell you. I promise."

She sank into a chair, feeling the weight of his words settle over her. The steady tick of the clock on the wall suddenly felt deafening. "What happened between you two?" she asked quietly.

There was another pause. "It was about Bigfoot," Bob admitted. "You know how he is about it. Always chasing something bigger, always out to prove the world wrong. It got to the point where... I couldn't be part of it anymore. He was so wrapped up in it that he stopped listening to reason. I told him I was done, and we haven't spoken since."

Emily closed her eyes, her frustration bubbling up alongside her fear. Of course it had been about Bigfoot. It always was. She had grown up watching her dad sacrifice everything for his obsession—friendships, money, his health. But he had always managed to come back, grinning like he'd found the edge of the map, certain he was just one step away from vindication.

Until now.

"He went off on his own, I'm guessing." Bob said, his voice hesitant. "He used to joke about keeping things under wraps so no one could steal his glory."

Emily's stomach churned. "He didn't tell me where he was going," she admitted. "Just that it was a cave system and that it was *the* place. He wouldn't even say what mountain."

Bob sighed again. "Damn. Sounds like him, alright." He hesitated, then added, "Look, if you want, we can meet up. Maybe I can help you figure something out. I know him better than most."

Emily glanced at the clock. The idea of sitting around, waiting for something—anything—to happen, made her chest tighten. "Yeah," she said. "I'll come to you. Where do you want to meet?"

"There's a diner just outside town, near Route 22. Eddie's Place. I'll be there in an hour."

"How about an hour and a half? I'm going to stop by his apartment and see if I can find anything that'll help me," she said, swallowing hard. "Thanks, Bob."

"Of course," he said gently. "We'll figure this out, Emily. One way or another."

She hung up the phone and stared at it for a long moment. Her father's voice echoed in her mind, from just yesterday morning:

"This is it. My moment. I'll be back before you know it."＊

But she didn't know it. She didn't know anything, and that terrified her.

———

The door to her dad's apartment groaned as Emily pushed it open, the faint scent of must and unwashed laundry hitting her immediately. She flicked on the overhead light, revealing a cramped, cluttered space. Papers and books covered every available surface, stacks of magazines teetered precariously, and the sink in the kitchenette overflowed with dishes crusted in old food. Her stomach turned.

"No wonder he never invited me over," she muttered, stepping carefully over a pair of muddy boots tossed haphazardly by the door.

The living room wasn't much better. A faded couch was buried under a mountain of newspapers and blankets, and a half-eaten sandwich sat forgotten on the coffee table, the bread curling at the edges. She ignored it and moved purposefully toward the door at the end of the short hallway. His office.

The room was worse than she'd feared.

The desk was covered in a chaotic sprawl of notes, photographs, and coffee-stained notebooks. A corkboard on one wall bristled with thumbtacks and pinned clippings from various sources: articles about wilderness sightings, blurry black-and-white photographs of supposed Bigfoot tracks, and a grainy image of a shadowy figure half-hidden among trees. A dusty filing cabinet stood in one corner, drawers pulled out and overflowing with more papers and folders.

On the wall above the desk was a large map.

Emily stepped closer, heart thudding with a flicker of hope. The map showed the Sierra Nevada mountain range in intricate detail, its peaks and valleys marked with winding trails and forested expanses. But as her eyes scanned it, her hope deflated. There were no marks, no pins, no circles drawn in red pen—nothing to indicate where her dad had gone.

"Damn it, Dad," she said under her breath. Always the paranoid one. He hadn't trusted anyone with his findings, not even her.

Her gaze fell to the desk. She began rifling through the mess, but it was overwhelming. There was no organization, no system. Just years' worth of research piled on top of itself. Notes on cryptid sightings were mixed with receipts and scraps of paper scrawled with illegible handwriting.

She shoved the papers aside in frustration, her hands trembling. "How was I supposed to find anything in this?" she said aloud, the sound of her own voice breaking the oppressive silence.

Her anger surged. She wanted to scream at him for being so reckless, for not telling her where he was going. He had always been like this—guarded, secretive, and convinced the world was out to discredit him. And now he was missing, and she was left standing in the middle of his chaos, helpless.

She looked around the room, desperate for any clue she might have missed, but the mess blurred together, an incomprehensible labyrinth of her father's obsession. Tears prickled her eyes, and she swiped at them angrily.

Turning back toward the door, she paused in the kitchen. The fridge was covered with magnets and scraps of paper—grocery lists, outdated coupons, and yellowing notes. But her eyes caught on a photograph, faded and curling at the edges, stuck to the fridge with a cheap magnet shaped like a bear.

It was of her and her dad, taken years ago. They were sitting on a log by a campfire, her dad's arm slung around her shoulders as she grinned at the camera. She could still remember the trip—the crackle of the fire, the smell of pine, the way her dad had laughed and told stories about the stars.

Her chest tightened as she pulled the picture free. It felt so far away now, like it belonged to someone else's life. She stared at it for a long moment before slipping it into her pocket.

"Let's go, Emily," she whispered to herself. She had to meet Bob, even if she still didn't know where to start looking.

She stepped out into the cool evening air, shutting the door to the apartment behind her. As she made her way to her car, the photograph pressed against her thigh felt like both a weight and a promise.

———

Eddie's Place was dimly lit and sparsely populated, the kind of diner where the coffee was always lukewarm and the air always smelled faintly of grease. Emily pushed open the glass door, the small bell above it jingling softly. Bob was already there, seated in a corner booth with a mug of coffee in front of him.

He looked up as she approached, his face worn and haggard. His once-dark hair was streaked with gray, and deep lines etched his features. He gave her a faint smile, but it didn't reach his eyes.

"Hey, kid," he said, standing awkwardly as she slid into the booth across from him.

She wanted to cry. The weight of the last 24 hours pressed heavily on her chest, and for a moment, she thought she might lose it right here in the middle of the diner. But she clenched her jaw and held it together.

Bob raised a hand to flag down the waitress. "Get her a coffee, would ya, Janie? On me."

Janie, a woman in her fifties with a pencil tucked behind her ear, gave Emily a kind smile and nodded.

"Thanks," Emily muttered, wrapping her hands around the laminated menu in front of her even though she wasn't hungry.

Bob leaned back, studying her. "You look like hell."

"Gee, thanks," she shot back, though her voice lacked venom.

He chuckled dryly, then grew serious. "Did the stop by his apartment bring any clues?"

She shook her head, her fingers tightening around the

edge of the menu. "He told me he was going out for the day. Said you were going with him. I've been trying to call him, but he's not answering. I went to his apartment, and... it's a mess, Bob. His office is a disaster. I don't even know where to start looking for clues."

The waitress returned with her coffee, setting it down in front of her with a clink. Emily murmured her thanks but didn't touch it.

Bob sighed, rubbing a hand over his face. "I wish I could tell you where he is, but I don't know. Like I said, we had a falling out months ago. Last time I saw him... well, it wasn't exactly on good terms."

"What happened?" she asked, her voice tight.

Bob leaned forward, resting his elbows on the table. "We had a fight. A big one. I'd been with your dad through thick and thin, helped him chase down leads, sift through reports, even interviewed witnesses with him. But it got to be too much, Emily. He was consumed by this... obsession. It cost him his marriage, his job, even his friendships. Hell, you've seen what it's done to him."

She nodded silently, staring into the dark swirl of her coffee.

"I told him I couldn't keep doing it," Bob continued. "I wanted him to let it go, at least a little. To think about his health, his relationships, his life outside of Bigfoot. But he just got angry. Told me I didn't understand, that I was giving up on something important. That this was his life's work."

Emily bit her lip, her throat tightening.

Bob shook his head. "He mentioned a spot, though. Said he thought he'd found it—the place. A series of caves, somewhere remote. He said it was near a hub of sightings, even missing person cases. He was so damn sure it was the real deal."

"Did he say where?" Emily asked, her voice sharp with urgency.

"Not exactly," Bob admitted. "You know how he was— always paranoid someone would swoop in and steal his discovery. All he told me was that it was remote. He said it'd take four hours on a quad just to get there. That's all I know."

Emily leaned back, her mind racing. A four-hour ride on a quad meant it wasn't another state—he was nearby. The Sierra Nevada mountains were vast, but if he was close to Truckee, that narrowed it down a little. The problem was the wilderness started just minutes outside of town. He could be anywhere.

Bob studied her expression. "Look, Em. I think you should go to the sheriff's department. File a missing person's report. They'll know what to do, and they've got the resources to help."

She hesitated, then nodded slowly. "You're right. I'll do that first thing."

Bob gave her a small, reassuring smile. "Good. And you're not in this alone, okay? You need help going through his stuff, you call me. We'll figure out where he went."

"Thanks, Bob," she said softly. She slid out of the booth, pulling her coat tighter around her shoulders. "Stay close to your phone. I'll call if I find anything."

"You got it," he said, raising his coffee mug in a mock salute.

As she stepped out into the cool evening air, the weight

of what lay ahead pressed down on her. She would go to the sheriff, but she knew deep down that the real work would fall on her shoulders. Her dad's office, chaotic as it was, held the answers. Somewhere.

She just had to find them.

CHAPTER 2

The sheriff's department sat on the edge of Truckee's small downtown, a squat, brick building with a handful of patrol cars parked out front. Emily stepped out of her car and glanced at the picture in her hand—a photo of her dad, taken last Christmas, his face lined but smiling warmly. She tucked it into her jacket pocket and marched up the steps.

Inside, the fluorescent lights buzzed faintly, and the smell of stale coffee hung in the air. A receptionist sat behind a desk, typing away on an old typewriter.

"Hi," Emily began, her voice steady despite the nervous energy churning in her stomach. "I need to file a missing person report."

The receptionist barely looked up, pointing her toward a deputy standing by the coffee machine. Emily approached him, clearing her throat. "Excuse me, Deputy—"

"Wells," he said, glancing at her before taking a long sip of coffee. "What can I do for you?"

She pulled out the photograph and placed it on the counter. "My father, John Hadley, hasn't come back from a trip. He left yesterday morning and hasn't answered any calls. I'm worried something's happened to him."

Wells frowned, picking up the picture. "John Hadley... isn't he that Bigfoot guy?"

Emily stiffened. "He's a cryptozoologist, yes, but that's not the point. He's missing, and I think he might be in serious trouble."

"Hmm." Wells set the picture down and scratched his chin. "Maybe he just decided to stay out a little longer. He's a grown man; he can take care of himself, can't he?"

Her temper flared, but she kept her tone even. "My father is in poor health, and he didn't tell anyone exactly where he was going. He mentioned something about remote caves—"

"Caves?" a new voice interrupted. Emily turned to see Sheriff Carter emerging from his office, his broad shoulders filling the doorway. His eyes narrowed as he stepped closer. "John Hadley's out chasing Bigfoot again, is he?"

Emily's jaw tightened. "Sheriff Carter. I just need someone to take this seriously. He's missing, and I—"

"I'll stop you right there, Miss Hadley," Carter said, crossing his arms. "Your father and I have history, and I'm not inclined to waste department resources chasing down another one of his wild goose chases. You know how many times he's come in here, spinning stories about Bigfoot and missing hikers?"

Emily's hands balled into fists. "This isn't about his work. This is about him being *missing*. Doesn't that matter to you?"

"It would," Carter said, his voice hardening, "if I

thought he was really in trouble. But the man's got a habit of going off the grid. He'll turn up when he's ready."

Carter wasn't completely off as John had two times before taken long unannounced trips where people have no idea where he was only for him to show back up.

"Unbelievable," Emily muttered under her breath, snatching the photo back from Wells. She turned on her heel and stormed out of the building, her heart pounding with a mix of anger and despair.

The cool evening air hit her as she stepped into the parking lot. She had barely reached her car when she heard someone call her name.

"Emily, wait!"

She turned to see Evan Morgan jogging toward her. He was dressed in the tan uniform of a deputy, his dark hair shorter than she remembered but his face just as familiar. She hadn't seen him in years, not since high school, when their brief relationship had fizzled out in the chaos of graduation and life pulling them in different directions.

"What do you want, Evan?" she asked, her voice clipped.

He slowed to a stop, hands on his hips as he caught his breath. "Look, I heard what happened in there. Carter's… well, he's stubborn. But I want to help."

She raised an eyebrow, crossing her arms. "Really? Why?"

He hesitated, then shrugged. "Because I know your dad's not just some crackpot, no matter what Carter says. And because I know you. You're not the type to panic over nothing."

Emily sighed, the fight draining out of her. "I don't know where to even start, Evan. His office is a mess, and the only thing I have to go on is something vague about caves and sightings. He didn't tell anyone where he was going."

"Then we start with what you have," Evan said simply. "I'm off duty in an hour. I can swing by and help you dig through his stuff."

She hesitated, studying him. Part of her wanted to refuse—this was personal, and she wasn't sure she wanted Evan involved. But she couldn't deny she needed help.

"Fine," she said. "I'm going back to his apartment now. Be there after your shift. It's the Timberwood Apartments off…"

"I know where they are."

"Of course you do. Apartment 2C."

Evan nodded, a small smile tugging at his lips. "I'll see you then."

Emily climbed into her car and drove off, her mind racing. Her dad's apartment loomed in her thoughts like a puzzle she didn't know how to solve.

———

Emily stepped back into her dad's apartment, the musty air and clutter greeting her like an unwelcome host. It was exactly as she had left it—papers strewn across every surface, dishes piled high, and the faint, sour smell of neglect hanging in the air. She wrinkled her nose and set her bag down by the door.

If she was going to make any progress, she needed to clear some space to work.

Under the sink, she found a roll of trash bags, dusty and shoved behind an assortment of half-empty cleaning supplies. Pulling one free, she set to work.

The dining table was her first priority. She swept away crumpled papers but not before ensuring they didn't hold clues, empty coffee cups, and even an old pizza box that was starting to grow spots of mold. The work was tedious, but it gave her something to focus on, keeping the rising tide of anxiety at bay. As she cleared the table, she muttered to herself, "How did he even live like this?"

Soon, a small pile of semi-organized notebooks and loose papers began to form on the cleared surface. She caught glimpses of her dad's scrawled handwriting: dates, coordinates, descriptions of sightings. Some of it was fascinating, but most was incomprehensible—a tangle of theories and cryptic notes that only made sense in his singular mind.

She had just started wiping down the table when a knock sounded at the door. Straightening, she brushed her hair out of her face and opened it to find Bob standing there, a brown paper bag in his hand.

"Thought you might be hungry," he said, holding up the bag. "Stopped by Miller's Burger Shack on my way over."

Behind him, another figure emerged—Evan. He gave her a tentative smile, one hand tucked into his pocket.

"Ran into this one on my way in. Figured you summoned him for extra help," Bob said, stepping inside.

Emily glanced between them, her exhaustion warring with gratitude. "Come in. The more hands, the better."

As Bob set the food on the counter, Evan took a look

around and let out a low whistle. "Your dad's office always look like this?"

"Probably," Bob said dryly. "You should've seen his garage. This is tame by comparison."

Emily shot them both a look but couldn't help the small smile tugging at her lips. "Alright, if you're here to help, grab a trash bag. I'm trying to get the table clear so we can go through his notes."

"On it," Evan said, rolling up his sleeves.

The three of them set to work, and the mess slowly began to shrink. Evan hauled the overflowing trash bags to the dumpster outside while Bob sorted through the stacks of books and papers, occasionally muttering under his breath about her dad's organizational "system."

"Found his old thermos," Bob said at one point, holding up a battered steel container. "Bet he didn't clean it out, either."

"Don't open it," Emily warned, laughing despite herself.

By the time they'd finished, the dining table was clean, and the rest of the apartment looked marginally less like a disaster zone. They sat around the table, digging into the burgers and fries Bob had brought.

As they ate, Emily pulled one of her dad's notebooks from the pile and flipped it open. The handwriting was cramped and uneven, as though he'd written in a hurry.

"This one's dated a few weeks ago," she said, scanning the pages. "He mentions sightings near Truckee, but nothing about specific caves. Just... references to 'the site' and 'finally finding it.'"

"That sounds like him," Bob said, taking a bite of his

burger. "He never wrote anything down in plain English. Always afraid someone would get their hands on it."

Evan leaned over, glancing at the notebook. "What about these numbers? Could they be coordinates?"

Emily squinted at the page. "Maybe. They're not labeled, though. They could just as easily be measurements or dates."

Bob reached for another notebook, thumbing through it. "If he was onto something, it'd be in here somewhere. He always left breadcrumbs, even if they were hard to follow."

For the next hour, the three of them sifted through journals, loose papers, and old files. Most of it was a jumble of notes and theories—pages filled with sketches of footprints, witness accounts, and maps of wilderness areas.

"This is going to take forever," Emily muttered, rubbing her temples.

"We'll get there," Evan said, his tone reassuring. "We'll figure it out."

Bob nodded. "Your dad might've been a stubborn old fool, but he was thorough. Whatever he was working on, he didn't just leave it to chance. There's a trail here, even if it's buried under all this."

Emily looked between them, a flicker of hope stirring in her chest. For the first time since this ordeal had started, she didn't feel entirely alone.

———

Hours passed, and the three of them worked tirelessly, their focus unwavering as they sifted through John Hadley's labyrinth of notes. Yet for all their effort, there was nothing

23

—no clear lead, no definitive answer to where he had gone. The frustration was palpable, hanging in the air as the pile of notebooks and papers seemed as endless as the wilderness John had ventured into.

Bob let out a long sigh, stretching his back as he stood. "I hate to say it, kid, but I've gotta call it a night. If I'm not home soon, Denise is gonna murder me in my sleep."

Emily gave him a faint smile. "Thanks for helping, Bob. I really appreciate it."

He nodded, grabbing his jacket from the back of a chair. "We'll find something. Your dad didn't do anything without leaving breadcrumbs, even if it's buried under all this crap." He gestured to the chaos on the table. "Call me if you find anything. And keep Evan on his toes—he's got young energy to burn."

Evan smirked. "Young? Well, I might be 28 but I feel 48, old man."

Bob grinned, tapping his temple. "I am an old man but I like to think my old age gave me wisdom and this belly," He said patting his stomach. He gave Emily and quick hug, turned, and headed for the door. "Night, you two." He waved as he left, the door clicking shut behind him.

Emily and Evan exchanged an awkward glance, suddenly aware of the silence that had descended in Bob's absence. For a moment, neither spoke, and then Emily cleared her throat. "Well, back to it, I guess."

"Yeah," Evan said, grabbing another notebook from the pile.

They worked in companionable silence at first, the occasional rustle of pages breaking the quiet. But exhaustion soon gave way to casual conversation.

"Remember how we used to get into trouble in Mrs. Jenkins's class?" Evan asked, a sly grin tugging at the corner of his mouth.

Emily laughed softly, her hands flipping through a folder. "How could I forget? You were always the instigator."

"Me?" he said, feigning innocence. "You were the one passing me notes with terrible drawings of her."

"Hey, those were masterpieces," she teased, smirking.

The conversation drifted, peppered with laughter and the occasional quip about their past. For a little while, the weight of the search lifted, replaced by the familiarity of two people who once knew each other well.

Evan glanced at the clock and sighed, closing the notebook in his hands. "I should probably head out too. Early shift tomorrow."

Emily hesitated, then asked, "Hey, before you go... how are you? I mean, it's been years since we've seen each other. You seem... good."

Evan gave her a small smile, leaning against the edge of the table. "I'm good. Life's not perfect, but whose is? Work keeps me busy, and I've been helping out my mom more since my dad passed last year."

Her expression softened. "I'm sorry to hear about your dad."

"Thanks," he said, his voice quiet. He glanced down at his hands, then back at her. "What about you? Still living in the city?"

"For now," she replied. "I needed a change after every-thing with my last job. This isn't exactly what I had planned, but... I guess I'll be here for a while, especially now."

He nodded, studying her for a moment. "You seem... different. More confident, I guess."

Emily smiled faintly. "Life does that to you."

The pause that followed stretched just a little too long. Then, trying to keep her tone nonchalant, she asked, "So... are you seeing anyone?"

Evan shook his head, his smile turning a bit shy. "Nope. Been too busy, I guess."

Her chest tightened slightly, though she kept her expression neutral. "Well, that's... good. For me, I mean. You seem like you've got a lot going on."

"Yeah," he said, straightening. "Guess I do."

They exchanged another awkward smile before Evan grabbed his jacket. "Alright, I'll let you get some sleep. Don't stay up too late digging through this mess."

"I'll try," she said, walking him to the door.

As he left, he turned back for a moment, his hand on the frame. "Call me if you need anything, okay?"

"Okay," she said softly.

The door closed behind him, leaving her alone in the quiet apartment.

She turned back to the pile of notebooks on the table, her exhaustion pressing down on her. But she couldn't stop. Not yet. With a sigh, she grabbed another notebook and began flipping through it, scanning for anything that might give her a lead.

Her eyelids grew heavier with each page, the words starting to blur together. Before long, her head sank onto the table, and the apartment grew still, save for the steady sound of her breathing as she finally drifted into a restless sleep.

CHAPTER 3

A heavy knock at the door jolted Emily awake. She blinked groggily, the dim morning light filtering through the blinds. Her neck ached from the awkward angle she'd fallen asleep at the table, surrounded by a sea of notebooks and papers.

The knock came again, more insistent this time. She stumbled to the door, still shaking off the remnants of sleep, and opened it to find an older woman standing there. The woman had a sweet smile and carried a small stack of mail in her hands.

"Good morning, dear," the woman said, her voice warm and friendly. "Sorry to bother you so early. I'm Mrs. Lockwood—live just down the hall."

Emily blinked, taking a moment to place the face. "Oh, hi. I'm Emily."

"I know," Mrs. Lockwood said with a knowing smile. "You're John's daughter, aren't you? Haven't seen you in years. Last time must've been when you were in college."

"Yeah, it's been a while," Emily admitted, rubbing the back of her neck.

The older woman held out the stack of mail. "This is John's. The mailman left it in my box by mistake yesterday. Thought I'd bring it over."

"Thank you," Emily said, taking the mail.

Mrs. Lockwood hesitated, her brow creasing slightly. "Is John off on one of his adventures again? Seems like I haven't seen him around in a couple of days."

Emily hesitated, the weight of her worry settling back onto her shoulders. "We're not sure where he is," she admitted. "He was only supposed to be gone for a day, but it's been more than that now. We're trying to figure out where he went."

The older woman's expression softened with concern. "Oh dear. That doesn't sound like him. He always comes back, doesn't he?"

Emily forced a small smile. "He usually does." She didn't want to go into the few times he did stay out past his scheduled return time.

Mrs. Lockwood tilted her head, her voice gentle. "I wish I could help, but I don't know where he might've gone. He always kept to himself about his work."

"It's okay," Emily said, clutching the mail. "Thanks for bringing this over."

"Of course, dear," the older woman said, patting Emily's arm lightly. "If you need anything, just let me know."

Emily nodded, watching as Mrs. Lockwood shuffled back down the hall. Closing the door, she tossed the stack of mail onto the table, adding it to the chaos she'd been working through the night before.

Her head still felt heavy from sleep, and she decided coffee was the only thing that could fix it. She rummaged through the small kitchenette, opening cabinets and drawers, but came up empty-handed. No coffee, no filters, not even instant. She groaned, leaning against the counter.

Another knock startled her, and she froze for a moment before heading back to the door.

This time, it was Evan. He stood in the doorway holding two steaming cups of coffee, a wry smile on his face.

"Figured you might need this," he said, handing her one of the cups.

She took it gratefully, the warmth of the cup seeping into her hands. "You have no idea how badly I needed this. Thank you."

Evan chuckled and stepped inside, glancing at the table covered in papers. "Looks like you had a long night."

"You could say that," she replied, taking a long sip of coffee. The bitter liquid jolted her awake a little more. "I didn't find anything. Just… more questions."

"Mind if I help?" he asked, gesturing to the table.

She shook her head. "Be my guest. At this point, I'll take all the help I can get."

Evan set his coffee down and grabbed a stack of papers, thumbing through them as he settled into a chair. Emily sat across from him, her eyes scanning the mail Mrs. Lockwood had dropped off. She began sorting the junk flyers and bills into small piles on the cleared dining table. Most of it was the usual clutter—credit card offers, grocery ads, a notice about expired insurance. She was just about to toss another nondescript envelope into the junk pile when the return address caught her eye: *Hobart Mills Property Management Company.*

She frowned. Hobart Mills was a small area just outside

of Truckee, a cluster of old cabins and rugged trails. She hadn't heard her dad mention anything about it before. Carefully, she tore open the envelope and pulled out the single sheet of paper inside.

It was a bill.

Her eyes scanned the page quickly:

Billing Statement

    Property Address: Lot #17, Pine Hollow Lane

    Balance Due: $450.00

    Description: Cabin rental fee, overdue.

She stared at the page, her mind spinning. *A cabin?* He'd never mentioned owning or renting one. She had no idea he'd even been to Hobart Mills recently.

Evan's voice pulled her out of her thoughts. "Something interesting?"

She held up the letter. "It's from a property management company in Hobart Mills. It's a bill for a cabin. He never mentioned it."

Evan leaned over to glance at the letter. "Hobart Mills? That's pretty remote. A lot of people rent cabins up there for hunting or getting off the grid."

Emily's stomach churned. "Do you think this could have something to do with where he went missing? Maybe the cabin is near those caves he talked about."

Evan shrugged, his brow furrowed in thought. "It's possible. If it's his, we should check it out. There might be something there—maps, notes, supplies. Hell, maybe he went there before heading to the caves."

Emily nodded slowly, her pulse quickening. "It's a lead. It's better than anything else we've found so far."

Evan straightened, setting his coffee cup on the table. "You want to go now?"

Emily hesitated. Her exhaustion tugged at her, but the thought of waiting any longer while her dad was still out there was unbearable. She met Evan's gaze, determination hardening her voice.

"Let's go."

Evan grabbed his jacket and phone as Emily stuffed the letter into her pocket. Together, they left the apartment, the stack of unanswered questions on the table growing smaller in the face of this new, tangible lead.

As they stepped into the crisp morning air, Emily couldn't help but feel a flicker of hope. If this cabin was connected to her dad's disappearance, it might finally point them in the right direction—and closer to finding him.

CHAPTER 4

John Hadley awoke to the suffocating chill of damp stone pressing against his cheek. His head throbbed, and his body felt heavy, every muscle aching as if he'd been crushed under the weight of the mountain itself. He tried to sit up, but his limbs were unresponsive, sluggish as if disconnected from his mind.

His fingers twitched, brushing against the wet, slimy ground. The smell hit him next—a stench so foul it made his stomach lurch. Rot, decay, and something else—musky and animalistic. He gagged, clamping a hand over his mouth as bile rose in his throat.

Where am I?

His heart pounded as fragmented memories flickered through his mind: the cave entrance, the footprints, the growl. And then... nothing. Had the excitement or terror caused his weak heart to skip a beat?

He blinked into the darkness, but it was impenetrable, like he'd been swallowed by the earth itself. His glasses were still on his face, but the left lens was cracked, distorting what little he could see. Panic clawed at his chest. He was alive, but he had no idea how long that would last.

"Hello?" he croaked, his voice hoarse and trembling. It echoed faintly, swallowed by the cavern's depths.

There was no answer.

He shifted, forcing his body into a crawling position. His hands slid across the wet, gritty surface, and he winced as sharp fragments bit into his palms. Bones. They had to be bones. He traced one with trembling fingers, its brittle surface cold and smooth. It felt human.

"Jesus," he whispered, jerking his hand back.

The smell grew worse as he moved, the stench thickening the air like a toxic fog. He gagged again but pressed forward, dragging himself inch by inch through the muck. His clothes were soaked, clinging to his skin, and he felt the unmistakable chill of his own filth adding to his discomfort.

He had to find a way out.

As he crawled, his hand brushed against something different—soft, damp, and yielding. He recoiled instinctively, his mind screaming at him not to think too hard about what it might have been.

Then he saw it—a faint glow ahead, like the promise of salvation.

Light!

Adrenaline surged through him, and he scrambled toward it, his knees and palms slipping in the mud. The air seemed fresher near the glow, less oppressive, and his lungs burned as he inhaled deeply.

The light grew brighter, revealing jagged rocks and patches of moss. He could make out the faint outline of the cave's entrance in the distance, an arch of freedom. Relief flooded his chest, momentarily overwhelming the pain and fear.

But then he saw it.

A shadow moved, massive and deliberate, blocking the faint glow from the cave entrance.

John froze, his breath catching in his throat. Slowly, he tilted his head upward, squinting through his cracked glasses.

The creature stood before him, its towering frame illuminated by the dim light. It was covered in dark, matted hair, its shoulders broad and powerful. Its chest rose and fell with heavy, deliberate breaths, and its eyes gleamed like coals in the dimness.

John's mouth went dry as he took in the creature's face. It was both alien and familiar, with a flat nose, deep-set eyes, and a wide, menacing jaw. Thick, gnarled hands hung at its sides, the fingers tipped with claws that glinted faintly.

For a moment, neither moved.

The creature stared down at him, its breath rasping, its presence filling the cavern with a sense of raw, primal power.

"Dear God," John whispered, his voice barely audible.

The beast crouched slightly, its massive head tilting as if studying him. Then, with terrifying speed, it reached out.

John flinched, but there was nowhere to go. The creature's hand clamped around his coat, lifting him effortlessly like a rag doll. He tried to struggle, but his limbs were weak, his body too battered to resist.

"Please," he gasped, his voice breaking. "Please, no..."

The beast said nothing, its heavy breaths the only

response. It turned and began to drag him back into the depths of the cave, its grip unyielding.

The light faded with every step, swallowed by the encroaching darkness.

John clawed at the ground, his broken nails digging into the mud, but it was futile. The creature's strength was absolute, its purpose inscrutable.

As the darkness closed in around him, John could only pray that someone, somehow, would find him before it was too late.

CHAPTER 5

The tires of Evan's truck crunched over gravel as they pulled onto the winding road leading out of Truckee toward Hobart Mills. The early afternoon sun filtered through the pines, casting shifting patterns of light across the dashboard. Emily sipped her coffee, staring out the window as the town gave way to dense wilderness.

"You didn't have to take time off for this, you know," she said, glancing at Evan.

He smirked, keeping his eyes on the road. "I didn't. Today was already my day off."

"Oh," she said, feeling a little foolish.

"And even if it wasn't," he added with a shrug, "I wouldn't mind. Your dad's been good to me in the past. Besides, you could use the backup."

She smiled faintly. "Well, thanks for coming anyway. I know it's not exactly your typical day off."

"Hey, I've had worse. Plus, it's not every day I get to catch up with an old friend." He shot her a quick grin, and for a moment, it felt like they were back in high school, sitting in his old beat-up Jeep, laughing about nothing.

The truck hit a small bump, and Emily gripped the armrest. She wasn't used to mountain roads anymore, but Evan seemed perfectly at ease, navigating the twists and turns with one hand on the wheel.

"So," he said, breaking the silence, "what's new with you? Last time I saw you was... what, graduation day?"

Emily nodded. "Yeah, I think so. Feels like a lifetime ago."

"It does," he agreed. "So? Fill me in. What's been going on in your world?"

She hesitated, then sighed. "Not much lately, honestly. I moved to the city after college, got a job, climbed the ladder a bit. For a while, I thought I had it all figured out. Then, about a year ago, things kind of fell apart."

Evan glanced at her, his brow furrowing. "What happened?"

"I had a serious boyfriend. We were together for a few years—almost got engaged, actually. But it just... didn't work out. We wanted different things." She shrugged, trying to sound nonchalant.

"I'm sorry," he said, his voice soft.

"It's fine," she said quickly. "Better to figure it out before walking down the aisle, right?"

He nodded, his hands tightening on the wheel. "Yeah, I guess so."

"What about you?" she asked, turning the question back on him. "I can't imagine you've been single all this time."

Evan chuckled. "Not quite. I had one serious girlfriend a few years ago, but it didn't last. She didn't like how much time I spent on the job. Said I wasn't committed enough."

Emily raised an eyebrow. "That doesn't sound like you. You were always one of the most dedicated people I knew."

"Yeah, well," he said with a shrug, "maybe I was too dedicated to the wrong things. It's not that I'm afraid of commitment or anything. I'm just... waiting for the right one to come along, I guess."

Her stomach fluttered unexpectedly, but she pushed the feeling aside.

"You're such a romantic," she teased, smirking.

He laughed, the sound warm and easy. "Guilty as charged."

They fell into a rhythm of conversation, trading stories and memories from their past. Emily told him about the time she accidentally set off the fire alarm during her first job, and Evan shared a story about a particularly embarrassing rookie mistake he made during his early days as a deputy.

"Wait, wait," Emily said, laughing so hard she could barely speak. "You're telling me you arrested the wrong guy because you misread the description?"

"Hey, it wasn't my fault!" Evan protested, grinning. "The guy matched the description *perfectly*. Besides, he was really understanding about the whole thing."

"Oh, I'm sure he was," she said, wiping a tear from her eye.

As the conversation flowed, Emily found herself relaxing for the first time in days. She hadn't realized how much she'd missed this—just talking, laughing, and being in the moment.

"I forgot how easy you are to talk to," she said softly, staring out the window.

Evan glanced at her, his expression warm. "Same here. I'm glad I'm here with you, Em. Feels like old times."

She looked over at him, his face illuminated by the golden sunlight streaming through the trees. He looked older, more filled out, and the years had added a quiet strength to his demeanor. He wasn't just the boy she'd dated in high school—he was someone more confident, more grounded.

"I'm glad too," she said, meaning it.

For the rest of the ride, their conversation ebbed and flowed naturally, the miles melting away as they shared pieces of themselves. Emily found herself thinking that if nothing else, she was grateful Evan was here now, keeping her grounded when everything else felt so uncertain.

As they approached the outskirts of Hobart Mills, the truck dipped into a shadowy grove of towering pines. The cabin wasn't far now, and Emily's stomach tightened with anticipation.

"Almost there," Evan said, his tone shifting to something more serious.

"Yeah," Emily said, her gaze fixed on the road ahead. Whatever they found at the cabin, she knew one thing for sure: she wasn't alone in this.

———

The cabin came into view as Evan's truck rounded the final bend in the gravel road. It was a small, weathered structure, its wood darkened by years of exposure to the elements. The roof sagged slightly in places, and the windows were streaked with dirt and grime. A narrow porch stretched across the front, its railing warped and splintered, with an old rocking chair sitting motionless in the breeze.

Emily's eyes immediately went to the truck parked out front—a battered blue pickup she recognized as her father's.

"That's his," she said, pointing as Evan pulled up and parked behind it.

Evan shut off the engine and leaned forward, squinting through the windshield. "Well, if his truck's here, the trailhead can't be far. That's a good sign."

Emily nodded, her stomach tightening with anticipation. They stepped out of the truck, gravel crunching underfoot as they approached the cabin.

The air was heavy with the scent of pine and damp earth, and the surrounding forest seemed to press in close, its shadows deep and impenetrable. Emily hesitated at the front door, testing the knob.

"Locked," she said, glancing at Evan.

"Let's check around back," he suggested, already moving toward the side of the cabin.

They followed a narrow dirt path that led to the rear of the cabin. The back door was slightly ajar, its hinges rusted and squeaking faintly in the wind. Evan exchanged a glance with Emily before stepping forward and pushing it open.

"Hello?" he called, his voice echoing inside.

No response.

Emily followed him in, her heart pounding. The interior

was cramped and sparse, with a small kitchen to the left and a sitting area to the right. A table near the window was cluttered with papers, notebooks, and an old camping lantern. A single cot with a thin blanket was pushed against the far wall, and a wood-burning stove sat cold in the corner.

"This is definitely his," Emily murmured, stepping closer to the table. The clutter was unmistakably her father's—a chaotic arrangement of maps, scribbled notes, and open books.

Evan nodded, scanning the room. "Looks like he's been here for a while."

They began sifting through the papers, their movements hurried but deliberate. Emily found sketches of footprints, detailed descriptions of sightings, and diagrams of the surrounding area.

"Over here," Evan said, holding up a map.

Emily joined him, her eyes widening as she saw the faint pencil marks etched across the surface. A circle was drawn around an area deep in the forest, with coordinates scrawled in the margin.

"This has to be it," she said, her voice trembling with excitement.

Evan nodded. "If he was going to the caves, this is where we'll find them. We'll need quads to get there, though. Looks like it's pretty remote. And today's our lucky day as I have a couple back in Truckee. I can go get them and trailer them back."

"How long will it take you?" she asked.

"By the time I get back, it'll be too late to start today, but we can hit the trailhead first thing tomorrow morning."

Emily nodded, grateful for his practicality. "I'll stay here, then. Keep looking for clues. And if he comes back…"

"You'll be here," Evan finished. He gave her a reassuring smile. "I'll be back as soon as I can."

As he left, Emily turned her attention back to the table, determined to make the most of the time she had. She sifted through more papers until her hand fell on a battered notebook, its cover smudged with dirt. Opening it, she saw her father's handwriting, scrawled and uneven, but unmistakable.

The entries were recent.

"I've been watching the cave for days now. It's more than I ever could have hoped for. Tracks leading in and out, massive and fresh. The creature—whatever it is—appears nocturnal. I've only caught glimpses, but it's real. It's so real I can hardly believe it. It's tall, well over eight feet, covered in dark fur. Its movements are deliberate, almost intelligent."

Emily's breath caught as she read on.

"Last night, it returned to the cave carrying something. I couldn't see what—too dark. But the way it moved… it's a predator. I'm certain now. *I have to get closer. I have to know for sure."*

The next entry was more hurried, the handwriting barely legible.

"Tomorrow is the day. I've mapped the caves as best I can from the outside, but I'll need to go in. If I can find evidence—hair, scat, anything—they'll have to take me seriously. This is my moment. If anyone finds this, I hope they'll understand what this means to me. What it could mean for all of us."

Emily closed the journal, her hands trembling. She set it down and looked toward the door, her father's words echoing in her mind.

Tomorrow is the day.

———

Evan pulled into the driveway of his modest house on the edge of Truckee, the trailer for the quads parked neatly to one side. He killed the engine, stepped out of the truck, and rolled his shoulders, stiff from the drive. The cool late afternoon air was bracing, carrying the faint scent of pine.

He unlocked the garage, the metallic clink of the padlock echoing in the stillness. Inside, two quads sat ready, their tires coated with a thin layer of dust from lack of use. He smiled faintly, patting the nearest one. "You're gonna earn your keep tomorrow," he muttered.

As he reached for the straps to secure the first quad to the trailer, the faint red light of his answering machine caught his attention through the window of the house. He hesitated, then stepped inside, curiosity tugging at him.

The machine blinked with urgency, the small number "3" glowing red.

"Three messages? Well someone must need me." Evan pressed the play button not sure of what to expect but assumed it was probably telemarketers which he'd been receiving recently since he placed his number in a drawing last month.

Instead, the gravelly voice of Sheriff Carter filled the room.

"Evan, it's Carter. I know it's your day off, but we've got a situation. A teenager's gone missing near Hobart Mills—was riding his mountain bike and didn't come back. His parents are raising hell. We need all hands on deck. Call me back as soon as you get this."

The message ended with a sharp click.
The second message immediately played.

"Evan, it's Carter, again. We need all hands on deck. Call me back as soon as you get this... forget that, just get your ass in here."

Evan sighed, running a hand through his hair. He

stopped the machine from the other message cause he knew who it would be. The timing couldn't have been worse. He glanced at the phone, debating whether to go in or let it go. Emily was counting on him, and he wasn't about to leave her hanging.

Still, he knew better than to ignore Carter outright. He picked up the receiver and dialed the dispatch number. After two rings, a familiar voice answered.

"Truckee Dispatch."

"Hey, it's Deputy Morgan," Evan said. "I got a message from the sheriff, but I'm tied up. Is there anyone else who can cover the missing kid?"

There was a pause on the other end, followed by a faint rustling. *"Hold on, Evan. Sheriff's on the line."*

Before Evan could protest, Carter's voice came through, sharp and authoritative.

"Morgan, you're not blowing this off."

Evan sighed inwardly. "Sheriff, I'm in the middle of something. Can't someone else handle this?"

"No," Carter snapped. *"We're stretched thin as it is. This kid's parents are influential, and the last thing we need is another missing person case blowing up in our faces. I need you on this, now."*

Evan clenched his jaw, glancing out the window toward the quads. "I was planning to head out toward Hobart Mills anyway tomorrow morning. Can't this wait a few hours?"

"No, it can't," Carter said, his tone brooking no argument. *"If you're already near Hobart Mills, you're closer than anyone else. Get out there. Search teams are setting up at the ranger station. That's an order."*

The line went dead, leaving Evan gripping the receiver

tightly. He set it back on the cradle with more force than necessary and exhaled slowly.

He knew there was no getting out of this. Missing kids took priority over everything else, no matter how inconvenient the timing.

Grabbing his jacket, he glanced at the quads in the garage one last time. Emily wasn't going to like this, but he'd have to deal with that later. For now, he had a missing teenager to find.

As he climbed back into his truck and pulled out of the driveway, he couldn't shake the gnawing feeling in his gut. Hobart Mills. First John, now a kid. The area was starting to feel less like a coincidence and more like a problem.

———

The cabin was suffocatingly quiet after Evan left. Emily had spent the last few hours combing through her father's notes and journals, the pages spread out across the table in a chaotic sprawl. The light of the old camping lantern flickered faintly, casting shifting shadows that danced across the wooden walls.

The night outside was pitch black, the dense forest swallowing any trace of moonlight. Emily had lit a few candles in addition to the lantern, but their warm glow did little to chase away the oppressive feeling creeping in from the darkness.

She glanced at the old rotary phone sitting on the counter, the receiver slightly off-center on its cradle. She frowned as she didn't have his number nor did he have this one, so the phone was useless in some regards.

Her anxiety rose as Evan was supposed to be back by now, and the longer the silence stretched, the more anxious she became. The drive to Truckee wasn't long, but hauling the quads and returning was a time-consuming task. Still, he should have returned hours ago.

She got up and paced, hugging herself against the chill that seemed to seep through the cabin walls. Her eyes drifted to the window, where the curtains hung loosely over the glass. She hesitated, then pulled them back just enough to peer outside.

The forest loomed, a wall of black silhouettes and faint rustling leaves. For a moment, she thought she saw movement—something tall and impossibly fast darting between the trees. Her heart leapt, and she jerked the curtain shut again, her breath quickening.

"It's just your imagination," she whispered to herself.

She returned to the table, but her father's scrawled handwriting blurred on the page in front of her. She rubbed her temples, trying to focus, but her mind kept circling back to the shadows outside.

A sudden creak of the deck outside made her freeze.

Her head snapped up, and she strained to listen. The sound came again—slow, deliberate footsteps, the heavy planks groaning under the weight of something.

Her pulse thundered in her ears as she stood, her chair scraping loudly against the floor. She winced, the noise making her feel exposed.

"Evan?" she called out, her voice trembling.

Silence.

She grabbed the heavy flashlight sitting on the table, her hands shaking as she clicked it on. The beam sliced through the dim cabin, its light steady and reassuring. She took a hesitant step toward the door, each creak of the floorboards beneath her feet echoing in the stillness.

The footsteps on the deck stopped.

Her stomach tightened, dread clawing at her throat. She reached the door, her knuckles white as she gripped the handle. "Who's there?" she called, louder this time.

No response.

Her breath caught as the doorknob began to jiggle, slowly at first, then harder, as if someone—or something—was testing it.

"Evan?" she whispered, her voice barely audible.

The knob stopped moving.

She took a step back, her heart hammering. Her eyes darted toward the window, half-expecting to see a face peering in at her. Instead, she was met with darkness, the faint glow of the lantern reflecting off the glass.

Her pulse pounded in her ears as she waited, the silence stretching unbearably.

"Evan? Is that you?" she tried again, her tone laced with both hope and fear.

Nothing.

Her hand hovered over the doorknob, her grip on the flashlight tightening. "Whoever you are, you better get out of here," she said, her voice sharp now, fueled by a mixture of adrenaline and panic. "I'm armed, and I won't hesitate to use it."

For a moment, there was only silence. Then she heard it —the sound of footsteps again, this time retreating quickly across the deck and into the woods.

Emily's stomach twisted. She rushed to the window and

pulled the curtain back, shining the flashlight out into the night.

The beam swept over the deck, empty now, and into the dense forest beyond. The trees stood like silent sentinels, their shadows shifting in the wind. She could hear movement—a faint rustling in the underbrush, the sound of someone—or something—running deeper into the woods.

She squinted, trying to make out a figure, but it was too dark. Whoever—or whatever—it was had vanished into the trees.

Her breathing was shallow as she dropped the curtain and stepped back, her grip on the flashlight trembling.

"Who the hell was that?" she muttered to herself, her voice barely audible over the pounding of her heart.

She paced the small room, her mind racing. It could've been a trespasser, a local, maybe even a prankster. But it could also be connected to her father—or worse, the creature he had written about in his journal.

Emily sat back down at the table, forcing herself to breathe deeply. She couldn't let her fear paralyze her. She still hadn't found enough answers, and until Evan came back, she was on her own.

She glanced at the door again, her nerves still on edge. Whoever had been out there was gone—for now. But she couldn't shake the feeling that they'd be back.

She resolved to stay awake and keep working. There was too much at stake to give in to exhaustion now. The stack of notes and journals in front of her was her only connection to her father, and she wasn't going to let fear stop her from finding the truth.

Even as the hours dragged on and her eyelids grew

heavy, she kept the flashlight within reach, her ears tuned to every creak and whisper of the night outside.

When she finally dozed off, it was not a restful sleep. The creaks of the cabin and the shadows of her imagination followed her into uneasy dreams, leaving her on edge and more afraid than ever.

CHAPTER 6

"Let me go!" Jake shouted, his voice echoing in the cavernous space around him.

Jake had been riding his mountain bike down a narrow trail near Hobart Mills when everything went wrong. The last thing he remembered clearly was the feeling of something massive colliding with him—like a truck slamming into his side—and then darkness.

Now, Jake was being dragged across the cold, wet ground. His body scraped against sharp rocks and muddy patches, and the overpowering stench of decay filled his nostrils, making him gag. He struggled, kicking and clawing at the hand—or paw—that gripped his leg, but it was like fighting against steel.

"Let me go!" he again screamed out.

The creature didn't respond. Its strength was inhuman, its movements steady and unrelenting. Jake craned his neck, trying to get a glimpse of it, but all he could see was a hulking shadow against the faint glow of moss-covered walls.

As they moved deeper into the cave, the light faded entirely, leaving only the sounds of his own ragged breathing and the creature's heavy, deliberate footfalls. The damp air clung to Jake's skin, and every breath tasted like mildew and rot.

When the creature finally stopped, it flung Jake aside like a sack of potatoes. He hit the ground hard, the impact knocking the air from his lungs. Pain radiated through his ribs as he gasped for breath, unable to do more than curl up in the cold mud.

The creature lumbered away, its footfalls receding into the darkness. Jake lay still, every nerve in his body screaming at him to move, but his muscles refused to cooperate.

Then he heard it.

Breathing.

It was close—too close. A shallow, rasping inhale, followed by an exhale that stirred the damp air around him.

Panic surged through him, and he scrambled to his hands and knees, but his legs buckled beneath him. He collapsed onto his side, shaking uncontrollably.

"Stay away," he whispered hoarsely, his voice trembling.

Desperation clawed at his mind as he fumbled in his pocket, his fingers brushing against the cold metal of his small flashlight. With trembling hands, he pulled it out and clicked it on.

The beam of light cut through the darkness, revealing the horrifying scene around him.

Bones.

They were everywhere, piled high and scattered across

the cavern floor. Skulls, ribcages, femurs—all picked clean, their white surfaces gleaming in the dim light. Jake's stomach churned, and he let out a choked scream, his voice bouncing wildly off the walls.

Then something moved.

His flashlight beam darted across the room, catching a fleeting glimpse of a shadow shifting in the corner. Jake screamed again, his throat raw with terror.

"Relax!" a voice hissed.

Jake froze, the flashlight trembling in his hand. He swung the beam toward the sound, his heart pounding so loudly he thought it might drown out everything else.

The light landed on a face—human, gaunt, and lined with exhaustion. The man squinted against the glare of the flashlight, raising a hand to shield his eyes.

"Turn that thing off," the man said, his voice low and urgent.

Jake hesitated, then lowered the flashlight slightly, his breathing still ragged. "Who—who are you?"

The man took a cautious step forward, his movements slow and deliberate. "Name's John. John Hadley and what's your name?"

Jake blinked, the name sparking recognition in the back of his mind. His parents had mentioned John Hadley before —the Bigfoot guy, the crackpot.

"I'm...ah...Jake."

"You hurt?"

"I don't think so."

"So you're good, well as far as good can get," John quipped.

"Yeah, I… I guess so," Jake stammered.

John nodded grimly and sat down heavily on a nearby rock. "Well, welcome to the nightmare. You're lucky it just dragged you here. Could've been worse."

"What is that thing?" Jake asked, his voice shaking. "What does it want?"

John ran a hand through his disheveled hair, his eyes dark and sunken. "I've been trying to figure that out for days. Maybe longer—time's a blur down here. Best I can tell, it's territorial. Smart, too. Smarter than we've given it credit for."

Jake shuddered, glancing around at the bone-strewn cavern. "All these bones… it eats people?"

John's expression hardened. "Not always. Some of these are animals, but yeah, some are human. It's been picking people off for years. I've been tracking it. Thought I could prove it exists." He gave a bitter laugh. "Guess I got more than I bargained for."

Jake hugged his knees to his chest, his flashlight clutched tightly in his hand. "Why hasn't it killed us?"

John leaned forward, his elbows resting on his knees. "That's the big question, isn't it? Maybe it's saving us for later. Maybe it's just toying with us. Either way, we're still breathing, and that means we've got a chance."

Jake stared at him, his fear mingling with a flicker of hope. "A chance to do what?"

"To get out of here," John said firmly. "But we've got to be smart. That thing knows these caves better than we ever will. It hears everything. Smells every-thing. If we're gonna make it, we've got to outthink it."

Jake swallowed hard, his hands trembling. "I don't want to die here."

"You're not going to," John said, his voice steady and calm. "Not if I can help it."

For the first time since he'd been dragged into the darkness, Jake felt a glimmer of hope. It was faint, like the beam of his flashlight cutting through the pitch black, but it was enough to keep him going.

———

Emily jerked awake, the sound of footsteps crunching outside the cabin jolting her upright in her chair. Her heart thudded wildly, and for a moment, she thought it was a dream. But then she heard it again—slow, deliberate steps circling the cabin, growing louder as they neared the porch.

She froze, her eyes darting to the door. Her pulse pounded in her ears, and she grabbed the iron stoker leaning against the fireplace—a makeshift weapon, but it was heavy and sharp enough to do damage if needed.

The footsteps stopped, replaced by a faint scratching sound at the door.

Her fear turned to anger. It wasn't just terror that had been building inside her all night—it was frustration. Evan still hadn't returned, she couldn't reach anyone for help, and whoever this was had pushed her too far. She wasn't about to cower in the corner and let them torment her.

Her grip tightened on the stoker as she crept toward the door. "I'm armed," she called, her voice trembling but loud. "You better leave right now, or I'll defend myself."

There was no response, only the soft sound of movement as the intruder stepped off the porch and began circling the cabin again.

Enough was enough.

Taking a deep breath, Emily yanked the door open and darted into the night, the cold air biting at her skin. The beam of her flashlight swept across the forest, but she couldn't see anyone. The footsteps moved faster now, crunching through the brush around the side of the cabin.

Emily didn't hesitate. She rounded the corner, gripping the stoker tightly. The flashlight's beam caught a figure moving along the edge of the trees—a man.

"Stop!" she shouted, her fear giving way to fury as she charged forward.

The man turned, startled, and stumbled back. "Wait! Don't hurt me!" he cried, throwing his hands up as he fell to the ground.

Emily skidded to a stop, the stoker raised. "Who are you? What the hell are you doing here?"

"Please," the man stammered, his voice trembling. "I'm not here to hurt you. I swear. I'm just looking for John Hadley."

The name hit her like a slap, and she narrowed her eyes, keeping the stoker raised. "How do you know my dad?"

The man scrambled to his knees, his hands still raised. "I'm Bryce Lang. I host *Paranormal Frequencies* on public access radio in San Francisco. I've... I've been following your dad for years. He's been on my show a few times."

Emily stared at him, her flashlight revealing a wiry man in his late forties, with wild, unkempt hair and thick glasses that glinted in the light. His face was pale and drawn, but his expression was sincere—terrified, but sincere.

"You're the guy who's been stalking him," she said coldly, her knuckles whitening on the stoker. Her dad had mentioned in previous conversations with her that someone had been *pestering* him.

Bryce winced. "Stalking is such a harsh word. I... I prefer 'tracking.' Your dad's brilliant—one of the best cryptid researchers out there. And I think he's close to something big. Really big."

Her stomach twisted. "What do you know about my dad? Where is he?"

Bryce sat back on his heels, catching his breath. "Look, I didn't mean to scare you. I thought the cabin was empty, and I was trying to see if I could find any of John's notes. Last time we talked, he told me he was onto something huge—something that could prove everything we've been saying for years. I've been trying to keep tabs on him ever since. I... I think I might know where he went."

"You thought it was empty? You came earlier so you knew it wasn't."

"I, I, I thought maybe you had left so I thought..."

Emily lowered the stoker slightly, though she still didn't trust him. "Start talking. Now."

Bryce adjusted his glasses, his hands shaking. "A few weeks ago, John called into my show. He didn't say much, but he mentioned he'd found a site—a series of caves he thought were connected to a string of disappearances. He wouldn't give details, but I could tell he was excited. Obsessed, even. After that, he went quiet. Stopped answering my calls."

Emily's throat tightened. "And you've been following him ever since?"

Bryce nodded. "I was trying to figure out where he'd gone. I didn't mean to scare you—I swear."

"Well my dad is now missing!"

"He's missing?" Bryce gulped.

"What do you know?"

"Listen, I just want to help. If he's in those caves, he could be in serious trouble. That creature…" He trailed off, glancing nervously at the dark forest around them.

"What creature?" Emily demanded, her heart racing.

Bryce's voice dropped to a whisper. "Bigfoot!"

"So you're one of those bigfoot people."

"Hey, if he's missing there's a good chance the creature got him."

"Or he's hurt himself or maybe he had a heart attack!" she countered. "You do know he has a heart condition."

"He never mentioned it. All I know is John told me he thought the creature might be responsible for the missing people around this area for decades and now apparently, he's missing."

Emily lowered the stoker completely, her mind racing. Bryce might be unhinged, but his words echoed her father's notes too closely to ignore.

"You want to help?"

"Yes."

"Fine," she said, her voice steely. "You're coming with me. But if you try anything, you'll regret it."

Bryce nodded eagerly, scrambling to his feet. "Of course. Whatever you need. I just want to help."

As they stepped back toward the cabin, Emily couldn't shake the feeling that she was hurtling toward something she didn't fully understand—something her father had spent years chasing but might have never truly wanted to find.

———

The makeshift command post buzzed with activity, the hum of radios and clipped voices filling the cramped ranger station near Hobart Mills. Maps and charts were pinned to corkboards, and a whiteboard at the center of the room displayed the critical details:

Missing Person: Jake Collins. Age 15. Last seen: 2:30 PM.

Evan leaned against a table covered with gear—compasses, flashlights, and first aid kits—his arms crossed tightly over his chest. Around him, members of the search and rescue team reviewed their assignments, their faces tense but focused.

Sheriff Carter stood at the head of the room, barking orders as he pointed at the whiteboard. "We'll split into three teams and cover the trails leading out from Jake's last known location. Dogs will run the perimeter, and our air support's limited, so make every second count."

Evan cleared his throat, stepping forward. "Sheriff, we need to expand this search to include John Hadley."

Carter turned, his expression tightening. "This isn't the time for that, Morgan. We've got a missing kid to find."

Evan refused to back down, his voice firm. "Hadley's been missing for over two days. His truck is parked not far from Jake's last known location. It's not a coincidence."

"You're pushing your luck, Deputy. This isn't a monster

hunt. It's a missing persons case, and I'm not wasting resources chasing wild stories."

"This isn't about monsters," Evan said sharply, stepping closer. "This is about people. If John's out there and Jake's gone missing in the same area, they could be connected. If we ignore that, we're putting both of them at risk."

"I'm not doing this bullshit monster hunt again, John did this too us before. Now go do what needs to be done to find that boy."

Evan opened his mouth to tell him about where the caves were but before he could speak, Carter barked at him.

"Get back to work, now!"

Defeated, Evan turned around and went back to organizing his team.

———

The faint glow of dawn seeped through the curtains of the cabin, casting long shadows across the cluttered table. Emily sat with her arms crossed, her eyes fixed on Bryce as he paced back and forth. The iron stoker was still within reach, its cold weight on the floor a reminder of how this bizarre night had begun.

Bryce's words tumbled out in rapid succession, his hands gesturing wildly as he spoke. "I've been following John's work for years. He's the best there is when it comes to cryptids. Most of the people in this field? Hacks. But John, he's the real deal."

Emily didn't respond, her eyes narrowing as she studied him. Bryce looked every bit the obsessed enthusiast—his hair disheveled, his glasses smudged, his clothes rumpled.

But there was a spark of genuine conviction in his eyes, something she couldn't entirely dismiss.

He continued, oblivious to her scrutiny. "The last time I talked to him—on my show a few weeks ago—he was more excited than I'd ever heard him. He said he'd found something. 'The proof,' he called it. Said it would silence the doubters once and for all."

"That's it?" Emily asked, her tone rising. "He didn't give you anything more specific?"

Bryce stopped pacing and turned to her, his face serious. "If I knew where the caves were, don't you think I'd be out there right now?"

Emily sighed, running a hand through her hair. She glanced at the door, her stomach twisting. Evan still wasn't back, and the weight of his absence pressed heavily on her chest.

"Do you think it's real?" she asked softly.

Bryce tilted his head. "What do you mean?"

"The creature," she clarified, her voice barely above a whisper. "Do you think it's actually out there?"

He didn't answer immediately, his gaze dropping to the floor. "I've spent my whole life chasing stories about things that go bump in the night. Bigfoot, Chupacabra, Mothman —you name it. Most of it's noise, but this? This feels different. John was convinced. And if he's convinced, I'm convinced."

Emily rubbed her temples, her mind racing. Her father's journal entries had painted a vivid picture of the creature— its size, its intelligence, its territorial nature. And now Bryce was here, backing up her father's claims with stories of his own.

"What else did he tell you?" she asked, her voice firmer now.

Bryce resumed pacing. "He mentioned the footprints—huge, deeper than anything a man could leave. He'd tracked them to the cave entrance but wouldn't go inside until he had everything ready. He said he saw the creature once, just for a moment. It was watching him, studying him. He thought it was… testing him."

Emily's stomach churned. The idea of something so massive, so intelligent, stalking her father sent a shiver down her spine.

"And then what?" she pressed.

Bryce shrugged helplessly. "And then he went silent. Stopped returning my calls. I thought he was holed up here, preparing for the big reveal. That's why I came. To see if he left anything behind."

"Wait. How did you know about this cabin?" she asked.

"He brought me out here about a year ago. I knew this was his spot for research so I figured."

"So you knew about this place and I didn't. I'm his daughter and he didn't feel to let me know," she said a tone of frustration in her voice.

"Sorry," he replied sheepishly. "If it helps, he often spoke fondly of you."

She cut her eyes at him then glanced at the table, the mess of papers and notebooks her father had left behind. Somewhere in this chaos, the answer had to be waiting.

The first rays of sunlight broke through the window, casting a golden glow over the room. Emily stood and moved to the window, pulling back the curtain slightly. The forest beyond was bathed in early morning light, but the sight didn't ease her nerves.

"You okay?" Bryce asked, his voice softer now.

"No, Bryce, I'm not," she snapped, her eyes scanning the tree line. "Evan should've been back by now."

Bryce frowned. "Who's Evan?"

"A friend," she said quickly, letting the curtain fall back into place. "He went to Truckee to get the quads so we could go to the trailhead. But he hasn't come back, and I don't know why."

Bryce crossed his arms and his brows raised, "Trailhead?"

"Yeah, the trailhead that'll lead us to the caves."

"You know where they are?"

She faced him and flatly said, "Yes."

Bryce jumped up and exclaimed, "Let's go."

"With what?"

"I brought my Suzuki LT 230 out here, it's just up the road."

"I have no idea what that is. Can it take us both?"

"Yes, ma'am."

"I'm not ma'am, I'm younger than you." Emily rushed past him, grabbed her jacket, turned and said, "Let's go find my dad and see if this monster of yours actually exists."

————

The command post radios crackled with updates, dogs barked impatiently, and the tension in the air was palpable. Evan stood near the edge of the room, his jaw tight as he watched Sheriff Carter bark orders at a group of volunteers.

He couldn't shake the feeling gnawing at his gut. Time was slipping away, and every second counted.

Finally, he stepped forward, pulling the sheriff aside. "Sheriff, I need a word," he said, his voice low.

Carter turned to him, his expression impatient. "What is it, Morgan? We're in the middle of organizing a search for a missing kid."

"This is about the missing kid—and John Hadley," Evan said firmly. "I think I know where they might be."

Carter's eyes narrowed. "What are you talking about?"

Evan glanced around, making sure no one was listening, then leaned in. "Last night, I went with Emily Hadley to John's cabin. We found a map and coordinates he left behind. It marked a spot in the wilderness—some caves. John was convinced they were connected to the missing persons cases in the area."

"And you're just telling me this now?" Carter snapped, his voice rising.

Evan stood his ground. "I didn't have a chance to bring it up earlier. You were laser-focused on the boy."

The sheriff's face darkened, and he pointed a finger at Evan. "You withheld critical information during a search operation? Are you out of your damn mind? You could've cost us valuable time!"

"I was going to handle it this morning," Evan shot back. "I didn't know a kid was going to go missing last night, and I sure as hell didn't think you'd listen to me if I told you about some map John Hadley left behind."

Carter stared at him, his jaw clenching. "Where's this map now?"

"At the cabin," Evan said. "Emily stayed behind to keep looking for clues while I went to get the quads."

"Then let's go," Carter barked, grabbing his coat. "You're not keeping this from me any longer."

The two of them hurried to Carter's truck, the engine roaring to life as they sped down the gravel road toward the cabin. The tension in the cab was thick, neither man speaking as the forest blurred past them.

When they reached the cabin, the sun was climbing higher in the sky, casting long shadows across the clearing. Evan jumped out of the truck before it fully stopped, his boots crunching on the gravel as he rushed to the door.

"Emily?" he called, throwing it open.

The cabin was silent. The table was still covered in papers and notes, but Emily was gone.

Carter followed him inside, his gaze sweeping over the mess. "Where is she?"

"I don't know," Evan said, his stomach twisting. "She was here when I left. She wouldn't just take off."

The sheriff's eyes narrowed, and he strode to the table, rifling through the papers. "Where's the map?"

Evan moved to the table, scanning the scattered notes. His heart sank. The map wasn't there. "She must've taken it," he muttered, running a hand through his hair.

Carter cursed under his breath. "So let me get this straight. The one person who knows where we need to go is gone, and she's got the map?"

"Yes," Evan said tightly. "And if she went after her dad, she could be in trouble."

Carter glared at him. "This is a damn circus, Morgan. First Hadley goes missing, then a kid, and now his daughter. You'd better hope we find them before this blows up in our faces."

Evan ignored the jab, his mind racing. He glanced around the cabin, hoping for any sign of where Emily might have gone. The chair she'd been sitting in was pushed back, and her jacket was missing from the hook by the door.

"She wouldn't go far without a plan," he said, half to himself. "She knows how dangerous this is."

Carter grabbed the radio clipped to his belt. "Dispatch, this is Sheriff Carter. We've got a new development. Be on the lookout for Emily Hadley, she is likely in the Hobart Mills area. Over."

The radio crackled in response, but Evan barely heard it. His thoughts were on Emily, alone in the woods, heading toward a danger she couldn't fully understand.

"We'll find her," Carter said grudgingly, as though trying to reassure himself as much as Evan. "And when we do, she's got a hell of a lot of explaining to do."

Evan nodded, his jaw tightening. "Let's not waste time."

———

The quad jolted violently over a deep rut in the trail, and Emily clung to the seat for dear life. Her fingers gripped his jacket tightly as the machine bounced and skidded over the uneven terrain, its engine growling like an angry beast.

"Hold on tighter!" Bryce shouted over the roar of the quad, his voice tinged with both excitement and impatience.

"I'm trying!" Emily yelled back, her voice strained. She had never been on a quad before, and the experience was far from what she'd imagined. Every bump and dip sent shockwaves through her body, and she was certain her legs were going to give out from gripping the sides so tightly.

The trail was a mess of rocks, roots, and muddy patches, winding through dense trees that seemed to close in around them. Emily squinted against the wind, her hair whipping across her face as Bryce maneuvered the quad with surprising skill.

After what felt like an eternity, Bryce slowed the machine, pulling off the trail onto a small clearing over-looking a sprawling valley.

"We'll take a break here," he said, cutting the engine. The sudden silence was jarring, leaving only the sound of the wind rustling through the trees.

Emily practically fell off the quad, her legs trembling as she tried to stand. "Oh my God," she groaned, stretching her arms and wincing as every muscle protested. "How do people do this for fun?"

Bryce chuckled, climbing off the quad and pulling a folded map from his jacket pocket. "You get used to it. Besides, you survived, didn't you?"

"Barely," she muttered, rubbing her lower back.

She stepped toward the edge of the clearing, where the land sloped down into a vast, breathtaking valley. The morning sun bathed the area in golden light, illuminating the rolling hills and jagged peaks beyond. A river snaked through the valley floor, its surface glinting like silver in the distance.

Despite everything—the fear, the exhaustion, the uncer-tainty—Emily felt a moment of peace as she stared out at the view. The wilderness was wild and untamed, and for a brief second, it was hard to believe anything sinister could be lurking within it.

"It's beautiful," she murmured, almost to herself.

Bryce didn't answer right away, too engrossed in the map he'd spread out on the seat of the quad. He pulled a small, well-worn lensatic compass from his pocket, flipping it open and lining it up with the markings on the map.

"Yep," he said absently, his brow furrowing in concentration. "This is the right direction. We're getting close. The cave system John marked should be just beyond that next ridge." He pointed toward a cluster of dark, jagged hills rising from the valley floor.

Emily turned back to him, still catching her breath. "You sure?"

"Positive," Bryce said, holding the compass steady. "The terrain matches his notes. If we keep going for another couple hours, maybe less, we should hit the entrance."

Emily's stomach twisted. The idea of being that close to the caves—her father's last known destination—filled her with equal parts dread and determination.

"Good," she said, brushing her hands on her jeans. "Let's get this over with."

Bryce looked up from the map, his expression serious. "You know, once we get there… it might not be what you're expecting. John was chasing something dangerous. If it's real, we're walking right into its territory."

Emily swallowed hard, her gaze drifting back to the ridge in the distance. "I don't care. My dad's out there somewhere, and I'm not leaving until I find him."

Bryce nodded, folding the map and slipping it back into his pocket. "Alright, then. Let's move."

Emily climbed back onto the quad, wincing as her sore muscles protested. She braced herself as Bryce started the engine again, the machine roaring to life beneath them.

As they pulled back onto the trail, Emily stole one last glance at the valley below, trying to hold onto the fleeting sense of calm it had given her. It wouldn't last—she knew that. But for now, it was enough to keep her going.

———

The quad came to a sputtering stop as Bryce cut the engine, the sudden silence pressing down on them like a heavy weight. Emily swung her leg over and stepped onto solid ground, her legs still aching from the brutal ride. She barely noticed the discomfort, her eyes locked onto the jagged rock formation ahead.

"This is it?" she asked, frowning as she took a few cautious steps forward.

The supposed cave entrance was sealed shut by a mass of massive boulders, wedged together so tightly that not even a sliver of darkness peeked through. The ground around it was disturbed, as if the rockslide had happened recently.

Bryce dismounted behind her, unfolding the map with hurried hands. "It has to be," he muttered, his eyes scanning the landscape. He pointed at the map, then at the rock wall in front of them. "The coordinates match, the terrain matches… but—"

"But there's no damn cave," Emily interrupted, hands on her hips.

Bryce turned to her, his expression tense. "It was here. It was open. Your dad marked this place for a reason."

Emily scowled at the blockade. The sheer size of the boulders was staggering—too massive to have simply collapsed on their own, unless an earthquake had triggered it. But she had checked the area for recent seismic activity before leaving. There hadn't been any.

"So what are you saying?" she asked, her frustration bubbling over. "That someone—or something—did this?"

Bryce ran a hand through his messy hair, exhaling sharply. "I don't know. But if John got in there, he didn't get out this way."

Emily stared at the sealed cave entrance, her pulse quickening. "Then we need to find another way in."

Bryce shook his head, eyes flicking between the map and the boulders. "Emily, we don't even know if there *is* another way in. This could've been the only entrance."

"You don't know that," she snapped.

"And neither do you!" Bryce shot back, his voice rising. "Look, I get it—you're scared, you're desperate. But running around blind out here isn't going to help."

Emily clenched her jaw, forcing herself to take a deep breath. She hated that he was right—hated that she felt so helpless standing in front of what should have been the answer. But she wasn't going to just stand here and do nothing.

Without another word, she turned and stalked off along the rock face, scanning the surrounding area for any sign of another opening.

"Emily!" Bryce called after her. "Where the hell are you going?"

"To find another way in," she yelled over her shoulder.

Bryce groaned and stuffed the map back into his pocket. "Jesus," he muttered before jogging to catch up.

She ignored him, moving quickly through the uneven terrain, her boots crunching against the dirt and loose gravel. The morning sun cast long shadows through the trees, making the rocks look even more menacing.

Bryce finally caught up, his breath coming in quick bursts. "You really think we're just gonna stumble across another cave entrance?"

"I don't know," Emily admitted. "But standing around arguing about it sure as hell isn't going to help."

Bryce exhaled through his nose, nodding reluctantly. "Fine. But let's not get separated, okay?"

Emily didn't answer. She was already scanning the cliffs, her heart pounding with renewed urgency. If this was the right place, if her father had come here, then there *had* to be another way in.

She just had to find it.

———

Evan trudged through the thick underbrush, his frustration mounting with every step. The sun was sinking fast, casting long shadows through the towering pines. His flashlight cut through the dimming light, sweeping across the forest floor, but there was nothing—no sign of Emily, no clue as to where she'd gone.

Beside him, Deputy Carl Grayson let out an irritated sigh. "I hate to say it, but this is like trying to find a damn ghost. She could've gone anywhere."

Evan didn't respond, his jaw tight as he pressed forward. The weight in his chest had only grown heavier since they'd left the cabin. He had checked for any kind of note, a clue, tire tracks leading in a clear direction—*anything* that would give them a lead. But the trails around the cabin all blended together, and once she had taken off, there was no way of knowing which direction she had gone.

"She couldn't have gone far," Grayson added. "Maybe she left something behind we missed."

Evan exhaled sharply. "We looked. The tracks from her quad lead into the woods, but once she hit the main trail, we lost her. Could've gone in any direction."

Grayson shook his head, adjusting the radio on his vest. "Damn it. If she got lost out here, we might not find her until morning."

That thought made Evan's gut twist. Emily wasn't reckless—at least, she never had been before. But desperation did strange things to people, and she was desperate to find her father.

Before Evan could respond, his radio crackled.

"Evan, you copy, it's the Sheriff."

Evan grabbed the radio. "Yeah, I'm here."

"Get back to base camp," Carter ordered.

Evan's stomach tensed. "Did you find something?"

An uncomfortable pause followed.

"Ahh, yeah we've got some new developments," Carter admitted. *"Nothing bad, but we need to regroup. We've got something lined up for morning."*

Evan exchanged a glance with Grayson before responding. "Copy that. Heading back now."

The walk back to the makeshift command post was tense, Evan's frustration growing with each step. When they arrived, the camp was buzzing with quiet activity—search teams were returning, some taking notes, others standing around talking in low voices.

Sheriff Carter stood near the main board, arms crossed, watching them approach.

"How'd it go?" Carter asked, though he didn't sound optimistic.

"Nothing," Evan admitted. "No tracks, no sign of her or anyone. It's like they all vanished."

Carter sighed, rubbing his temple. "Figured as much. We're running out of daylight, and if we keep pushing in the dark, we risk losing more people out there."

Evan clenched his fists. "So what's the plan? We can't just sit here."

Carter smirked slightly. "We're not. I pulled a favor. We've got a chopper coming in to assist with the search."

Evan blinked. "A helicopter?"

Carter nodded. "Truckee PD is sending one of their units. But it won't be available until first light."

Evan crossed his arms, his jaw tightening. "That's still hours from now."

"And it's better than nothing," Carter countered. "We'll cover more ground in ten minutes up there than you and Grayson did all day."

Evan exhaled through his nose. He knew the sheriff was right, but that didn't make waiting any easier. Every hour that passed was another hour Emily was out there alone, in the dark, heading straight toward the unknown.

Carter clapped him on the shoulder. "Get some rest, Morgan. We go again at dawn."

But Evan knew there wouldn't be any rest. Not until he found Emily.

The forest had swallowed them whole.

Night fell fast in the wilderness, the last streaks of twilight fading behind the jagged peaks in the distance. The temperature had plummeted, leaving Emily shivering in her thin jacket. She hadn't packed for this—hadn't thought about how cold the Sierra Nevadas got at night.

Bryce had stopped looking at the map an hour ago, his frustration mounting with every dead end. They had scoured the area, but the entrance to the cave system was either buried or hidden in a way they couldn't figure out in the dark.

Now, they were huddled under a towering pine tree, backs pressed against its rough bark, the world around them pitch black. Emily had never felt so exposed. The night seemed *alive*, filled with rustling leaves, distant cracks of branches, and the eerie stillness that only deep wilderness could bring.

Her breath came in shallow bursts, visible in the freezing air. "We should've brought camping gear," she muttered, hugging her arms tightly against her chest.

"Yeah, well, I didn't expect to be out here after dark either," Bryce said, rubbing his hands together for warmth. His voice was tight, and for the first time since they'd met, he seemed genuinely unsettled.

A long, eerie silence stretched between them before a distant sound broke it.

A low, guttural *whoop*.

Emily stiffened. "What the hell was that?"

Bryce didn't answer right away. His posture had gone rigid, and his head tilted slightly, listening. Another *whoop* came seconds later, this time from a different direction.

Then another.

It was distant but unmistakable—almost like a deep-voiced owl but more deliberate, more calculated.

Bryce swallowed hard. "That's—" He stopped himself, shook his head, and lowered his voice to a whisper. "That's not good."

Emily turned to him, her pulse thudding in her ears. "What do you mean 'not good'? What *was* that?"

Bryce wet his lips, scanning the darkness beyond them. "It's a call. A communication call."

Emily's stomach twisted. "Communication between *what*?"

Bryce inhaled deeply. "Bigfoot."

Emily opened her mouth to argue, to call it ridiculous, but she stopped herself. She had read her father's notes. He had written about sounds like this before—whoops, wood knocks, stone clacks—things he believed weren't random forest noises but an intelligent creature's way of signaling to others.

Another *whoop* sounded—closer this time.

Emily pressed herself further against the tree, her fingers digging into the bark. The darkness seemed thicker now, like it was closing in around them.

"You're sure?" she whispered.

Bryce nodded slowly, his breath shaky. "It's the same kind of call I've recorded before. And if we can hear it, that means *they* know we're here."

A cold dread settled over Emily's bones.

She had spent years rolling her eyes at her father's theories, dismissing his claims as delusions of an obsessed man. But now, sitting in the freezing dark, hearing something *she couldn't explain,* she wasn't so sure anymore.

A rustle sounded in the underbrush to their right.

Emily grabbed Bryce's arm instinctively. "Did you hear that?"

"I heard it," Bryce whispered.

They both sat frozen, barely breathing. The darkness beyond the trees was suffocating, hiding whatever was out there. They had no fire, no weapons, nothing but a flashlight, which neither of them dared to turn on.

More movement. Footsteps? Something heavier than a deer, slower than a bear.

Emily's hands trembled. "We should leave...," she whispered, barely able to get the words out. "...get back to the quad."

Bryce shook his head. "Good idea, just no sudden movements. If it's what I think it is, we don't want to act like prey."

Emily's heart pounded in her chest. The air was so thick with tension it felt like the forest itself was holding its breath.

The sound of another *whoop* echoed in the distance—this time, an answer.

Emily shut her eyes for a brief moment, then followed

Bryce closely praying that whatever was out there wasn't coming to get them.

———

The moment Emily saw the quad, her entire body surged with relief. They were exhausted, freezing, and rattled beyond belief, but they had made it back. All they needed to do was get on the damn thing and ride out of here. She hated leaving but whatever was out there was close by and they needed to go back, regroup, and come back with more people and some weapons.

Bryce scrambled forward, his boots skidding slightly in the loose dirt as he threw a leg over the seat. "Come on," he muttered, jamming the key into the ignition.

Emily climbed onto the back, gripping his jacket tightly as he twisted the starter.

Click.

The quad sputtered but didn't start.

"What?" Bryce twisted the throttle and hit the ignition again. The engine whined but refused to turn over.

Emily's stomach tightened. She turned and glanced back toward the trees, her breath coming in fast, shallow bursts. The night was eerily quiet. Too quiet. The distant *whoops* had stopped, and that was worse than hearing them.

It meant something was *here.*

"Bryce," she whispered, gripping his shoulder. "We need to go. *Now.*"

"I know that!" he snapped, his frustration mounting as he jabbed the starter again.

The quad coughed, sputtered, and fell silent.

Emily turned her head toward the woods. Shadows stretched between the trees, shifting with the wind, but she couldn't shake the feeling that they weren't alone. The hairs on the back of her neck stood on end.

Bryce slammed his fist against the handlebars. "It was fine when we got here! What the hell is wrong with it?"

"Try it again," Emily urged, barely holding onto her patience. Her heartbeat pounded so loudly it drowned out every rational thought.

Bryce yanked at the ignition one more time.

The quad roared to life.

"Yes!" Bryce shouted. He twisted the throttle, and the machine jolted forward, kicking up dirt and gravel as they shot down the trail, the headlight providing much needed illumination to the darkened forest.

Emily barely had time to lock her arms around his waist before they were speeding through the darkened forest, the roar of the engine filling her ears. The air was freezing against her exposed skin, her hands numb against the fabric of his jacket.

But they were moving. They were getting out.

Then something stepped onto the trail.

It happened so fast that Emily barely registered what she was seeing.

A massive figure, dark and hulking, moved out of the trees ahead of them.

It wasn't human.

It was *big*.

Glowing eyes caught the light from the quad's head-lamp, reflecting it back like twin embers in the dark.

Bryce let out a startled yell and yanked the handlebars to the right in a desperate attempt to avoid a collision.

The quad veered violently off the trail.

"Bryce—!"

The last thing Emily saw was the massive trunk of a pine tree rushing toward them.

Then impact.

The force of the crash was brutal.

Bryce was thrown forward like a rag doll, his body slamming into the tree with a sickening crack. His head connected with the trunk so hard that the sound of bone snapping echoed through the trees. He went limp immediately, crumpling like a marionette whose strings had been cut.

Emily was hurled sideways, her body ripped from the quad as she flew through the air.

She barely had time to process what was happening before she hit the ground hard, tumbling violently down a steep embankment.

Pain exploded through her body as she rolled uncontrollably, rocks and roots tearing at her clothes, her limbs flailing helplessly as gravity dragged her further into the abyss.

She hit the ground. Hard.

Her body slammed into a boulder at the bottom of the ravine. The impact forced the air from her lungs in a painful, strangled gasp.

Then everything faded to black.

The forest returned to silence.

Evan stormed into the cabin, his frustration mounting with every second. The old wooden door slammed shut behind him, the echo reverberating through the small, cluttered space. His flashlight cut through the darkness, illuminating the chaos that was John Hadley's research.

Emily was gone. No note, no obvious clue left behind. And without that map she had taken with her, he had nothing to go on.

He dragged a hand down his face, exhaling sharply before moving toward the table. The lantern still sat where Emily had left it, surrounded by stacks of notebooks, loose papers, and books on cryptozoology. It was a mess—but messes held secrets, and Evan needed to find one.

He grabbed the first notebook, flipping through the pages furiously. Nothing but old sighting reports, sketches of footprints, and theories on creature behavior. He tossed it aside and reached for another.

John's cramped handwriting covered the pages, notes scribbled in frantic excitement. Coordinates were jotted down in the margins, but they weren't detailed—no clear directions, no indicators of a specific location. Evan cursed under his breath and kept searching.

He moved to the cabinets next, yanking them open. Empty food cans, mismatched plates, a half-burned candle —nothing useful. He slammed the doors shut and crouched down, searching through the lower cupboards. His fingers brushed against something rough, shoved into the very back. He pulled it out.

A map.

His heart kicked up as he spread it out on the table, eyes scanning the marked trails and handwritten notations.

Some of the marks were old, faded from years of handling, but there were newer ones—places John had circled recently.

Evan leaned closer. One location stood out, a more defined marking compared to the rest. A rough note next to it read:

Cave entrance? More research needed.

His pulse quickened. This had to be it. The caves. The ones John had been obsessed with. The ones Emily had gone looking for.

Grabbing the map, he folded it roughly and stuffed it into his jacket pocket. He wasn't going to waste another second.

As he turned toward the door, something caught his eye —a small recorder sitting on the edge of the table.

Evan hesitated before picking it up. The plastic casing was worn, the buttons faded. He clicked the rewind button instinctively, then pressed play.

A crackle of static. Then, John's voice, slightly distorted but unmistakable.

"The sightings are too frequent to be coincidence. Something is out there. Tracks are fresh. The cave system is real —deeper than I expected. I think… I think it's watching me."

Evan's grip tightened around the recorder.

"If I disappear, it's not an accident. Someone—or something—doesn't want me here."

The recording cut off.

Evan clenched his jaw.

Emily was out there, chasing this same lead, walking straight into whatever John had been afraid of.

He had to find her. Now.

———

Emily drifted between the edges of consciousness, her mind caught in a hazy void. Pain radiated through her body in dull, throbbing waves, but it felt distant—like it belonged to someone else. Her breath was shallow, her chest rising and falling with effort.

Then she became aware of something above her.

Her eyelids fluttered open, her vision swimming, but she forced herself to focus.

A massive figure loomed over her, silhouetted against the night sky. Only the faintest slivers of moonlight illuminated its shape, casting jagged shadows across its hulking frame.

It was enormous. Broad shoulders, impossibly long arms, thick fur matted and dark. It stood still, watching her. The air was thick with the pungent scent of wet earth, musk, and something else—something almost rancid.

She tried to move, to shift even slightly, but her body refused to respond.

The figure exhaled heavily, its breath warm and damp against the cold night air.

Then darkness took her again.

———

She came to in motion.

Her head lolled against something firm and unyielding, the sway of movement lulling her back toward unconsciousness. But before she could sink fully into the void, her senses stirred.

The smell was overpowering—thick, animalistic, something between damp fur and rotting leaves. It clung to her skin, filled her nose, made her want to gag.

The thing carrying her was warm, its arms solid muscle beneath thick, coarse hair. They were huge, wrapping around her effortlessly, cradling her like she weighed nothing.

Emily's mind struggled to process what was happening. *This isn't real. This can't be real.*

She tried to lift her head, but the effort sent sharp pain lancing through her skull. Her vision blurred, the rhythmic thudding of massive footsteps reverberating through her body.

Then she was falling.

No—not falling.

Being lowered.

Her back hit a hard, damp surface, the cold seeping into her skin instantly. The scent of wet stone filled the air, mingling with the thick, organic musk of her captor.

Her breathing hitched as she tried to force her eyes open, to fight against the waves of unconsciousness pulling her under again.

Then she heard them.

Voices.

Low murmurs, hushed but urgent, echoing around her. More than one.

And then—one voice cut through the fog in her mind. A voice she had spent days searching for.

"Emily?"

Her breath caught.

Her father's voice.

"Dad…" she whispered, barely able to form the word before the darkness swallowed her again.

CHAPTER 7

The first thing Emily felt was cold. It pressed against her skin, seeped into her bones, made her shiver violently. The air was thick, damp, and heavy with the scent of wet stone, earth, and something more primal—something *wrong*.

Her eyes fluttered open, unfocused, the dim light doing little to help her disoriented mind. Shapes moved in the darkness. A voice—low, urgent—called her name.

"Emily?"

She tried to sit up, but pain shot through her body like fire. Her head throbbed, and her limbs felt like they were weighted down with lead.

"Take it easy," the voice urged, firm but gentle.

She blinked, forcing her vision to clear. A shadow hovered over her, a familiar face coming into focus beneath the flickering light of a small fire.

Her father.

"Dad?" her voice cracked, barely above a whisper.

John Hadley exhaled, his face lined with exhaustion but

filled with something else—relief. "Yeah, sweetheart. I'm here."

Emily struggled to process what was happening. She was lying on the cold, hard ground, her back pressed against damp stone. The cavern ceiling stretched high above her, jagged and uneven. Nearby, another figure shifted in the dim glow.

Jake.

The missing teenager sat hunched against the wall, his arms wrapped tightly around his knees. His face was pale, his expression hollow, his eyes wide with exhaustion and fear.

Emily tried to push herself up again, groaning as a sharp pain shot through her ribs. "Where are we?" she asked, looking between them.

John ran a hand down his face, sighing deeply. "The cave system. The one I was searching for." His voice was quiet but laced with a grim weight.

Emily swallowed hard, her memories coming back in flashes—the quad, the crash, the massive figure on the trail. The *thing* that had stepped in front of them. And then...

The creature.

Her eyes darted around the cavern, suddenly hyper-aware of the vast, echoing space around them. "Dad... tell me everything."

John hesitated, his eyes flickering toward the shadows that stretched beyond the fire's glow. Then he nodded, shifting closer.

"I've been looking for this thing for most of my life," he admitted, his voice low. "Ever since I first started tracking the sightings, I knew there was *something* out here. Something real." He glanced at Jake, then back at Emily. "But I never imagined this."

Emily's hands clenched into fists. "What is this?" she pressed. "What do you know about it?"

John took a slow breath. "It's big. Bigger than any human. Seven, maybe eight feet tall. Covered in thick, dark hair. But it's not just some dumb animal. It's smart. *Really* smart."

Jake shifted, his voice shaky. "It brought me here. I... I tried to fight, but it was too strong."

John nodded. "Same with me. It doesn't kill right away. That's what worries me."

Emily's stomach twisted. "So what does it do?"

John's jaw tightened. "I don't know." He looked toward the cavern walls, as if expecting something to be listening. "It hunts. It's territorial. It takes what it wants, but I don't know why it's keeping us alive."

Emily shuddered, hugging her arms around herself. "So what happens to us?"

John hesitated again. Then, finally, he met her gaze.

"I don't know for sure," he admitted. "But I do know one thing."

Emily swallowed hard. "What?"

Her father's face was grim, his voice barely above a whisper.

"We should be afraid."

Emily stiffened her spine and with bravado in her voice declared, "Someone is coming, I just know it."

———

Evan stormed into the command post, his boots kicking up dust as he moved with purpose. The inside of the makeshift HQ was buzzing with activity—search teams relaying updates over the radio, volunteers sorting through supplies, and Carter, standing over a large map of the region, barking orders to a few deputies.

Evan didn't wait for permission. He walked straight up to the sheriff and slammed a folded map and a handful of John Hadley's notes onto the table.

Carter barely looked up. "This better be good, Morgan."

Evan jabbed a finger at the map. "This is where they are."

That got Carter's attention. His eyes flicked to the map, taking in the hastily marked coordinates and the hand-written notes scribbled in the margins. "Where'd you get this?"

"Hadley's cabin," Evan answered. "It was buried under a pile of junk. It marks a cave system he was investigating —the one he was convinced was tied to the missing persons cases out here." He pointed at a circled location deep in the wilderness. "This is where he was headed, and if Emily was following his trail, this is where she is now."

Carter frowned, leaning over the map. "You're sure about this?"

"As sure as I can be," Evan said. "And I'm not waiting around for that helicopter. I'm taking a quad out there now."

Carter scoffed, crossing his arms. "You're not taking off on some half-baked rescue mission alone, Morgan. That's how people stay missing."

Evan clenched his jaw, his patience wearing thin. "Then

let me take a team. We've got extra quads. I'll take two people with me. We go now, and the second the chopper's in the air, you send it straight to these coordinates."

Carter stared at him for a long moment, clearly weighing the options. Then he sighed, rubbing his temple. "You're a pain in my ass, you know that?"

Evan didn't smile. "Yeah, I've been told."

Carter shook his head and gestured toward the supply tent. "Fine. You get two deputies, no more. Gear up, take what you need, and get moving. But if you're not checking in every hour, I'm sending people after you, got it?"

"Got it," Evan said immediately.

Carter pointed at the map. "And the second the chopper's ready, it's heading here. If you're in trouble, don't play hero—use the damn radio."

Evan folded up the map and stuffed it in his jacket. "I just want to bring them home."

Carter sighed again, waving him off. "Then get going."

Evan turned and strode toward the quads, his pulse pounding and his mind set on one thing—getting to Emily.

The search teams were still scattered throughout the command post, but he ignored the chaos and headed straight for the quad staging area. A few officers were working on refueling, but when they saw him approaching with purpose, they straightened.

"I need two of you," he said, his voice leaving no room for argument. "We're heading out now."

Two deputies exchanged looks before stepping forward. The first was Deputy Mark Reynolds, a solid, no-nonsense guy Evan had worked with for years. He was steady under pressure and didn't ask stupid questions—exactly what

Evan needed. The second was Deputy Linda Torres, a sharp-eyed officer who had a background in search and rescue. She was a damn good tracker, and Evan was thankful she had volunteered.

"Where are we going?" Torres asked, strapping on her radio.

Evan pulled out the map, unfolding it quickly. "We found this in Hadley's cabin. He marked a cave system deep in the wilderness. I think it's where he was heading, and I think Emily is there now."

Reynolds studied the map, nodding. "That's way out there. Terrain's gonna be rough."

"I don't care," Evan said. "We've got to move fast. The chopper's coming at first light, but we're not waiting for it."

Torres gave him a skeptical look. "Sheriff actually signed off on this?"

Evan smirked. "Not before giving me hell about it. But yeah, he's letting us go. We're taking three quads and as much gear as we can carry."

Reynolds grinned. "Guess that means we're in for a hell of a night."

Evan gave a single nod. "Let's gear up. We leave in ten minutes."

———

The roar of the quads echoed through the forest, their headlights cutting through the darkness as they barreled down the uneven trail. The cold night air bit at Evan's exposed skin, but he barely felt it—his adrenaline was running too high.

Torres was up ahead, leading the way. She had studied the map before they left, plotting the fastest route toward the caves. Reynolds followed close behind, his quad kicking up dirt and loose gravel.

Evan rode in the rear, eyes scanning the trees for anything unusual. The forest felt wrong—too quiet, too still. There were no distant animal calls, no rustling of small creatures in the underbrush. Just the sound of their engines and the wind whipping past them.

After nearly an hour of hard riding, Torres suddenly raised a hand, signaling them to stop.

Evan pulled up alongside her. "What is it?"

Torres pointed ahead. "Trail's too narrow from here. We're close, but we'll have to go the rest of the way on foot."

Evan shut off his quad and swung his leg over. "Then let's move."

Reynolds grabbed a rifle from his pack. "You think we're gonna need these?"

Evan's gaze hardened. "I don't know. But I'm not taking any chances."

They secured their gear and moved out, flashlights sweeping across the thickening trees. The terrain grew steeper as they climbed, the scent of damp earth and pine filling the air.

Then, just as they crested a ridge, Torres froze.

"Do you hear that?" she whispered.

Evan stopped, holding up a hand for silence.

At first, there was nothing. Just the wind through the trees.

And then—

A deep, resonant *whoop* echoed through the forest.

Torres swallowed hard. "Tell me that was an owl."

Evan's grip tightened on his flashlight. "It wasn't."

Another *whoop* came, this time from the opposite direction.

Reynolds took a cautious step forward. "We need to keep moving. We're almost there."

Evan nodded, his gut twisting. They had to get to Emily —now.

And whatever was out there?

It knew they were coming.

––––––

The damp air clung to Emily's skin, her breath coming in slow, steady pulls as she tried to ignore the way the darkness pressed against her from every direction. The only light came from the faint glow of bioluminescent fungi clinging to parts of the cave walls and the dying embers of the small fire John had managed to build. The cavern smelled of wet stone, mildew, and something deeper, something rancid that made her stomach churn.

They had been trapped down here for hours.

Emily sat up, her head still pounding from the crash, but her mind was clear enough now to know one thing: *They had to get out of here.*

She turned to her father and Jake, her voice low but firm. "We have to go. Now."

John sat against the wall, his eyes shadowed, weary. "We don't know the way out," he said. "And don't know where *it* is."

Emily clenched her fists. "Exactly. We haven't seen it for hours. That's our window. If we wait until it comes back, we might not get another chance."

John sighed, rubbing his forehead. "You don't understand, Em. This thing—this creature—it knows this cave better than we ever could. It's a predator, and we're in its den."

Jake, who had been silent, swallowed hard. "I don't want to die down here," he whispered. His voice cracked. "If there's even a chance we can get out, I say we take it."

Emily nodded, trying to keep her voice steady. "If we stick together, if we move fast and stay quiet, we can do this." She turned back to John, her eyes pleading. "Dad, please."

John hesitated, then exhaled sharply. "Alright," he said, reluctantly pushing himself to his feet. "But we move carefully. No sudden noises. No light unless we absolutely need it."

Emily nodded. "Agreed."

Jake let out a shaky breath, his hands trembling as he stood. "Which way?"

John hesitated before pointing toward a narrow tunnel leading away from the chamber. "I think that way slopes upward. If we keep following the incline, it could lead to an exit."

Emily didn't hesitate. "Then let's go."

―――――

They moved single file, their breathing shallow, the only sounds their cautious footfalls against the damp stone. The walls of the cave were slick with condensation, the air growing colder the deeper they went.

Jake clung to Emily's side, his knuckles white as he gripped a jagged rock for balance. Every few feet, he cast a glance over his shoulder, as if expecting to see something lurching from the shadows.

Emily felt it too.

That terrible presence—the sense that something was watching them, unseen but close.

As they pressed forward, they began to see remnants of what had come before them.

Bones.

Scattered across the cave floor, piled in corners, wedged between cracks in the stone.

John crouched next to a pile, examining a skull with careful hands. "Some of these are animal," he whispered, his voice barely audible. "But some aren't."

Emily didn't want to look, but she forced herself to. There was no mistaking it—humans had died down here. Some of the bones still had tattered shreds of clothing clinging to them.

Jake whimpered but kept moving.

Then, up ahead, Emily saw something else—a rusted, half-buried flashlight.

She picked it up, brushing away the dirt. It was old, corroded, but when she pressed the switch, it flickered weakly before dying.

"Someone else was here," she murmured.

John nodded grimly. "And they didn't make it out."

The terror clawed at Emily's stomach, but she pushed it down. *That won't be us.*

They kept moving.

The tunnel narrowed, forcing them to squeeze through jagged rock formations. At times, the only way forward was to crawl. The walls pressed in tightly, the air growing thinner, the silence deafening except for their own ragged breathing.

Then—far ahead—a faint sound.

Wind.

Emily's heart surged with hope. "Do you hear that?" she whispered.

John nodded. "Could be an opening."

Jake's breathing hitched. "We're almost out?"

John placed a hand on his shoulder. "Almost."

For the first time since waking in this nightmare, Emily felt a spark of hope. They were so close.

Then the air shifted.

A deep, low rumble echoed through the cave behind them.

John's face paled.

Emily turned, dread sinking into her bones.

The sound wasn't the wind.

The rumble turned into a growl. A deep, guttural vibration that reverberated through the walls, through their bones.

Then came the sound of movement. Heavy, deliberate footfalls echoing through the tunnels behind them.

Emily's breath hitched. *It's coming.*

"Go," John hissed. "Now!"

They ran.

The tunnel twisted and narrowed, their breath ragged, feet pounding against the uneven stone. The wind ahead was stronger now, promising an exit—but behind them, the beast was closing in.

A massive, guttural *whoof* sounded from behind, like air being forced from giant lungs. A shadow shifted in the darkness, moving faster than anything that big had the right to.

Jake screamed.

Emily turned, just in time to see him stumble.

His foot caught on a loose rock, and he tumbled forward, slamming against the cavern floor. His flashlight slipped from his grip, clattering into the darkness.

John skidded to a stop. "Jake, get up!"

Jake scrambled to his knees, his breaths coming in quick, panicked gasps. But before he could move, the shadows shifted behind him.

Emily's stomach dropped.

The creature was there.

A monstrous, hulking silhouette filling the narrow passageway, its massive shoulders scraping against the walls. The dim glow of bioluminescent moss caught in its fur, outlining its monstrous form—towering, covered in thick, matted hair, its chest rising and falling with slow, deliberate breaths.

Its eyes gleamed.

Jake found a rock, picked it up, turned, and hurled it at the creature, hitting it in its face. The rock simply bounced off like a pebble hitting a wall.

Jake's face turned ashen just as the creature lunged.

A single massive hand shot out, fingers closing around the boy's head like a vice.

Jake let out a strangled scream, his arms flailing wildly, his legs kicking against the ground.

Then—CRACK.

The sickening sound of bone shattering echoed through the cavern.

Jake's body went limp, his arms dropping to his sides. His legs twitched once, then stilled.

Emily clamped her hands over her mouth, a scream choking in her throat.

John grabbed her wrist. "Run."

They sprinted forward, the tunnel sloping sharply downward. The ground grew slick beneath their feet, and Emily nearly lost her footing as they barreled blindly through the dark.

Behind them, the creature let out a guttural snarl.

It was coming for them.

The tunnel walls closed in, forcing them to duck low as they ran. The wind howled now, a promise of open air, of escape. Emily's lungs burned, her body screaming at her to stop—but she couldn't.

Then the ground disappeared beneath her feet.

She fell.

A sharp scream tore from her throat as she plummeted into darkness, her arms flailing for something—anything—to grab onto.

She hit something solid—her father.

John grunted as they tumbled together, their bodies twisting and rolling down an unseen drop. The world spun, flashes of rock and darkness blending into chaos.

Then—*impact.*

Emily hit the ground hard, the air forced from her lungs in a brutal gasp.

She lay still, the cold stone pressing against her cheek, her ears ringing.

Somewhere above, the creature snarled, its heavy footfalls stopping at the edge of the pit.

Emily forced her eyes open, her breath ragged.

John lay beside her, groaning, one hand gripping his ribs. Blood trickled down his temple.

Above them, the darkness swayed. The beast was watching.

Waiting.

Trapped in the depths of the cave, Emily and John barely had time to process the nightmare they were in but her gut told her they were now trapped.

―――

The rising sun bled gold across the treetops as Evan and his team tore through the forest on their quads, the engines roaring in the crisp morning air. The oppressive darkness of the night had finally melted away, but even with the light breaking through the trees, there was a lingering sense of unease.

Then, up ahead—something on the trail.

Torres raised a hand, signaling for them to slow.

Evan pulled up beside her, his eyes locking on the sight just ahead. A quad sat abandoned on its side, the front end smashed against a tree, the handlebars bent at an awkward angle. A few feet away, sprawled at the base of the same tree, was a man's lifeless body.

"Shit," Reynolds muttered, already pulling his rifle, a Winchester Model 30-30, from long leather rifle holster strapped to the rear side of the quad.

Evan dismounted his quad quickly, jogging toward the wreckage with his heart hammering. He crouched beside the dead man, taking in the brutal injuries. His head was at an unnatural angle, the skull clearly crushed on impact. His clothes were disheveled, his boots muddy, and his glasses— cracked and askew—clung to his pale face.

"Who the hell is this?" Torres asked, standing over the body.

Evan scanned the area, his mind racing. "No idea. But if I had to guess, he was with Emily."

Reynolds frowned. "You think she was on that quad?"

Evan's stomach tightened as he studied the wreckage. The machine was big enough for two people, and there was no sign of a second body. That meant Emily had been with this guy, but she wasn't here now.

She had to be alive.

Evan stood, glancing around. "No blood trails, no drag marks. If she was injured, someone—or something—took her."

Torres exhaled sharply. "So what's the play? Keep moving?"

Evan pulled the map from his pocket, unfolding it over the seat of his quad. His finger traced over the notations John Hadley had made. "The cave system should be close. We have to be right on top of it."

Reynolds scanned the treeline, then nodded toward a small ridge up ahead. "That terrain matches Hadley's notes. If the caves are anywhere, it's there."

Evan shoved the map back into his jacket. "Then let's move."

The three of them moved cautiously now, their rifles at the ready as they pushed deeper into the woods. The rising sun cast long shadows over the land, but the sense of being watched hadn't gone away.

Then, just like that—the whoops stopped.

Torres looked around, gripping her rifle tighter. "Anyone else feel like we just crossed a line we weren't supposed to?"

Evan nodded, but he didn't say anything. He had felt it too.

Minutes later, they arrived at a massive rock formation, the same one Emily had found hours earlier. The boulders were piled high, an unnatural barrier sealing off whatever lay behind them.

"Jesus," Reynolds muttered, running a hand over the stone. "This was placed here."

Torres frowned. "By who?"

Evan had a sinking feeling he already knew.

"This has to be it," he said. "Hadley marked the caves right here."

Torres pressed a hand against the boulders. "So, what? If this was the way in, how do we get inside now?"

Evan took a deep breath, scanning the rock wall, the ridgeline, the surrounding trees. His pulse was steady, but his instincts screamed that they were running out of time.

"We split up," he decided. "One of us will find another way in."

Reynolds nodded. "I'll take the right side of the ridge. See if there's another entrance along the slope."

Torres adjusted the strap on her rifle. "I'll check along the tree line, see if there's an opening we missed."

Evan set his jaw. "I'll climb up, check the higher ground."

The three exchanged quick nods before splitting off.

Evan took one last look at the blocked cave entrance, his fists clenching.

Hold on, Emily. I'm coming.

———

Evan climbed steadily up the rugged slope, his boots scraping against loose gravel and damp earth. The higher he went, the more twisted the trees became, their roots gnarled and tangled as if resisting something unnatural buried beneath them. The morning light barely reached this far, and even though the sun was rising, the air felt colder here, heavier.

Then he saw it.

Just ahead, nestled between a jagged split in the rock face, was a dark opening. It wasn't large—just wide enough for someone to crouch and slip through. But it was definitely an entrance. The ground in front of it was disturbed, the dirt churned up as if something—or someone—had been dragged inside.

"Got something," he called down.

Reynolds and Torres were on him in seconds, both breathing hard from the steep climb.

"Jesus," Torres muttered, aiming her flashlight toward the gaping hole. The beam barely penetrated the darkness. "This has to be it."

Evan didn't answer. He already knew.

The smell confirmed it.

A putrid, overwhelming stench wafted out from the cave, making his stomach churn. It was a mix of rotting flesh, damp earth, and something worse—something rancid, primal.

Reynolds gagged, pressing a sleeve against his nose. "Oh, hell no."

Torres coughed, taking a step back. "That's... that's death."

Evan swallowed hard, forcing himself to breathe through his mouth. Every instinct screamed at him to turn around, but he ignored it. Emily was in there.

He pulled out his radio, clicking it to life. "Torres, get back to the quads. Radio Sheriff Carter. Tell him to proceed to the coordinates I left him."

Torres wiped at her mouth, still grimacing. "You sure?"

Evan nodded, his jaw tight. "Tell him we found an entrance. And tell him we found a body."

Torres cursed under her breath but didn't argue. She turned and started down the slope, moving quickly but cautiously.

Reynolds shifted beside Evan, his rifle raised. "This is bad."

Evan tightened his grip on his weapon, eyes fixed on the darkness ahead. "Yeah," he muttered. "But we're going in anyway."

Evan had brought headlamps with him. He handed one to Reynolds and they both put them on. They weren't bright but they would chase the darkness way.

The two men crouched, steeling themselves, and stepped into the cave with their rifles at the ready.

———

Emily's body ached in ways she had never experienced before. Every breath sent sharp, agonizing pain through her ribs, and she was certain at least one—probably more—was broken. Her head throbbed, her limbs felt like dead weight, and the damp chill of the cavern seeped into her bones.

But she wasn't dead.

And she wasn't going to just sit here and die.

She turned her head, wincing as she moved, and saw her father beside her. John Hadley was slumped against the rock wall, his arms limp at his sides, his face pale under the dim light filtering into the pit. His lips moved, but the words coming out were low, incoherent murmurs.

"The creature... the great unknown... magnificent..." He let out a breathy, almost reverent chuckle. "And here I am. In its grasp. I was right. I was right."

His voice cracked with something between awe and madness.

Emily pushed herself up onto her elbows, biting back a cry as pain flared in her side. She looked up. The creature was still there, perched at the top of the pit, its massive form backlit by the faint light from above. Its breathing was deep and steady, the rise and fall of its chest deliberate and powerful.

It watched them.

Emily held her breath.

Then—a sound.

A distant noise echoed through the cave, something further down the tunnels, something that made the creature tense. Its large, dark head snapped toward the source of the sound, its posture shifting from menacing to alert.

Then, without a second glance, it turned and sprinted into the darkness, vanishing in an instant.

Emily let out a shaky breath.

It was gone.

For now.

She turned back to John. He was still muttering, his fingers trembling, his wide eyes staring blankly ahead.

"I knew it would come to this," he whispered, chuckling softly again. "I always knew. The skeptics, the scientists, the government—none of them believed me. But I was right. And now I die at the hands of Bigfoot." His laughter deepened, but there was no joy in it. It was hollow, broken.

Emily's stomach twisted.

"No," she said firmly. "No, you are not going to die down here, Dad."

He didn't even acknowledge her.

"We have to move," she continued, gritting her teeth as she forced herself to sit up fully. "That thing isn't going to be gone for long. We have to climb out of here."

John didn't respond.

His eyes were unfocused, his breathing shallow. He had spent his whole life searching for proof of this thing, and now, faced with it in the worst possible way, something inside him had snapped.

Emily reached out and grabbed his arm. "Dad. Look at me."

Nothing.

"Dad!" she shouted, shaking him.

Still nothing.

Panic surged in her chest. She couldn't do this alone—she needed him to snap out of this.

Her hand trembled as she lifted it.

Then she slapped him across the face.

Hard.

The sharp crack of her palm meeting his cheek echoed in the pit.

John's head snapped to the side, and for a moment, there was nothing but stunned silence.

Then his eyes refocused.

He blinked, slowly at first, his breathing ragged. Then his gaze met Emily's, and something shifted—recognition. Awareness.

Emily's throat was tight, her voice shaking. "We are not going to die here."

John swallowed hard. He looked up at the steep walls of the pit, his lips parting slightly as if seeing them for the first time. Then he looked at her again—really looked at her.

And he nodded.

"Alright," he murmured, his voice hoarse. "Let's climb."

Emily exhaled in relief, shoving her pain to the back of her mind.

She could feel time slipping away, the creature still lurking somewhere in the tunnels.

They had to get out.

Now.

Torres crouched at the highest point of the ridge, gripping her radio tightly as she adjusted the frequency. The crisp morning air did little to ease the tension in her gut. The sun was up now, cutting away the suffocating darkness of the night before, but that didn't make this situation any less dangerous.

She pressed the button on her radio. "Sheriff Carter, this is Deputy Torres. Do you copy?"

Static crackled for a moment before Carter's voice came through, sharp and to the point. *"Go ahead, Torres."*

"We've located what appears to be an alternate entrance to the cave system," she said, scanning the rugged terrain below. "Morgan and Reynolds are already inside, searching for Emily Hadley. We also found an unidentified deceased male near a wrecked quad. Possible connection to Hadley. Over."

A long pause. Then Carter's voice returned, his tone harder. *"Torres, listen carefully. I need you to get back to Morgan immediately and tell him to stand down."*

Torres blinked. "What? Sheriff, they're already inside."

A beat of silence.

"I didn't ask if they were inside, Torres. I said get them out of there. Now."

Something about his voice made the hairs on the back of her neck rise.

"Understood," she said, keeping her tone neutral. "I'm heading down now."

She clipped the radio back onto her belt and took off down the ridge, her boots skidding slightly on the loose dirt. Something was wrong. Carter was holding something back, but now wasn't the time to question it.

When she reached the cave entrance, the stench of rot and damp earth rolled over her like a wave, making her stomach lurch. She pulled her rifle tighter against her chest and flicked on her flashlight.

"Evan! Reynolds!" she called, stepping inside. Her voice echoed through the cavern, swallowed by the suffocating darkness.

No answer.

Torres pushed forward, her pulse hammering in her ears.

She needed to find them. Fast.

———

Evan and Reynolds moved carefully through the cave, their flashlights cutting through the suffocating darkness. The deeper they went, the worse the stench became. It was an unbearable mix of rot, damp earth, and something sickly sweet, clinging to their nostrils and making their stomachs churn.

"This place is a goddamn tomb," Reynolds muttered, shifting the rifle in his grip.

Evan nodded grimly, his jaw tight. The cavern walls felt like they were closing in on them, their footsteps echoing in the vast emptiness. Every so often, a faint drip of water somewhere in the distance reminded them they were deep beneath the earth, far from the safety of the outside world.

Then the beam of Evan's flashlight caught something ahead.

A body.

Sprawled out on the cave floor, motionless.

Both men stopped cold.

Reynolds swallowed hard. "Jesus."

They approached slowly, weapons at the ready. The closer they got, the worse the sight became. The body was twisted unnaturally, arms sprawled, legs bent at an odd angle. The head… or what was left of it… was barely intact, shattered like a melon.

Evan exhaled sharply. "It's the kid."

Reynolds took one look at the remains, stumbled backward, and bent over, vomiting onto the cave floor. The sound echoed grotesquely in the stillness.

Evan kept his eyes locked on the corpse, his stomach twisting into knots. Jake Collins. The missing teenager. He had hoped—prayed—that they would find him alive.

But they were too late.

Reynolds wiped his mouth, breathing heavily. "What the hell did that?"

Evan already knew. And he had a feeling they were about to find out.

"Let's keep moving," he muttered, stepping over the body and pressing deeper into the cave.

The smell thickened, the walls growing narrower. The ground beneath them was slick, almost muddy, and the air felt alive, like it was breathing with them.

Then, they turned a corner.

And there it was.

The massive creature stood just a few yards ahead, hunched slightly beneath the cave ceiling, its broad, muscular form covered in thick, matted hair. Its eyes—small, dark, and intelligent—gleamed as it fixed its gaze on them.

A deep, guttural growl rumbled from its chest.

Evan barely had time to react before it moved.

Faster than he ever thought possible, the creature lunged.

Evan yanked his rifle up, but before he could fire, a massive, clawed hand swung.

The impact hit him square in the chest, sending him flying backward. His body crashed against the jagged cave wall, the breath ripped from his lungs.

Blackness swarmed his vision. His limbs went slack. The world spun.

Somewhere in the haze of his fading consciousness, he heard Reynolds shout.

Then, the sickening sound of bones snapping.

Evan forced his eyes open just in time to see the creature gripping Reynolds by the throat, lifting him effortlessly off the ground.

Reynolds struggled, his boots kicking at the air, his hands clawing at the massive fingers around his neck. His rifle dangled uselessly from its strap, his grip completely lost.

The creature squeezed.

A wet, grisly *crunch* filled the cavern.

Reynolds' body jerked violently, then went limp.

With a grunt of disgust, the creature tossed the deputy's lifeless form aside like a broken doll. The body crumpled to the cave floor, motionless.

Evan groaned, rolling onto his side. Pain flared through his ribs and shoulder, but adrenaline shoved it aside. He reached for his rifle—just a few feet away—his fingers brushing against the cold metal.

Then he heard it.

A scream.

"HELP!"

Emily.

She was alive.

Evan's pain disappeared in an instant. He pushed himself to his feet, stumbling toward the sound, ignoring the rifle he had been about to grab.

He ran.

The creature turned, locking its gaze onto him again.

For a brief moment, Evan thought it was about to chase him—but then, something else caught its attention.

A voice.

"MORGAN, REYNOLDS!"

Torres.

She was calling from the near the entrance of the cave, her voice echoing through the tunnels.

The creature growled, turning toward the sound, nostrils flaring.

Then, with an almost deliberate choice, it turned away from Evan and stormed toward the direction of Torres' voice.

Evan didn't waste time questioning why.

He sprinted toward Emily's scream, deeper into the abyss.

———

Torres moved carefully through the entrance of the cave, her rifle raised, her flashlight cutting through the thick darkness ahead. The smell hit her immediately—rotting, damp, unnatural. She swallowed hard, forcing herself to breathe through her mouth, but the rancid stench still clung to the back of her throat.

She took another cautious step forward, her boots crunching against loose gravel. The air in the cave was heavy, pressing down on her like a physical force. She could hear the faintest sounds—dripping water, the distant scuttling of small creatures—but nothing human.

Then—a gunshot.

The sound shattered the silence, echoing violently through the tunnels.

Torres' breath hitched. "Evan?" she called out, her voice tight, cracking slightly.

Silence.

She gritted her teeth, her grip tightening on her rifle. *What the hell was happening in here?*

Her mind raced. Should she press on? Or should she turn back and radio for Carter, tell him they needed backup now?

She exhaled sharply, standing frozen, debating with herself.

"This is stupid," she muttered under her breath, her voice barely above a whisper.

She wasn't trained for this—search and rescue, sure. Backwoods police work, sure. But this? Chasing something that felt *wrong*? That smelled of death? That didn't belong in any rational world she understood?

She bit her lip, shifting her weight.

"Alright, Torres," she murmured to herself. "Get your ass in gear or get the hell out of here."

But she couldn't decide. She stood there, paralyzed by fear, her flashlight trembling slightly in her grip.

Then she heard it.

Thud.

Her breath caught.

Thud. Thud.

It was distant at first, but it was growing louder. Closer.

Someone was running toward her.

Her heartbeat slammed in her chest.

She raised her rifle, pointing her flashlight straight down the tunnel.

The beam of light revealed something massive, something wrong.

A towering figure, covered in thick, dark hair, barreling straight toward her at terrifying speed.

Its footfalls were like thunder, shaking the ground beneath her. Its eyes glowed, catching the reflection of her light, deep and dark and filled with intelligence.

Torres' breath left her in a sharp, panicked gasp.

The flashlight slipped from her fingers, clattering to the floor.

She turned and ran.

Her boots pounded against the stone, her lungs burning, her body screaming at her to move faster. The dim light from the cave entrance was ahead—a beacon of escape, salvation. *If I can just make it outside—*

But she didn't.

Just as she reached the threshold of the cave, something massive slammed into her back.

A scream tore from her throat as she was lifted off the ground, a crushing force wrapping around her midsection.

The world spun violently as the creature swung her through the air like a rag doll.

Her body smashed against the cave wall, pain exploding through her ribs and back. Then she was yanked backward and hurled again.

Her shoulder cracked against solid stone, her skull bouncing off the rock. Her vision went white with agony, her limbs going numb.

She barely had time to process the pain before she was slammed down against the hard ground, the impact knocking the breath from her lungs.

Her head lolled to the side, her vision blurry, her body refusing to respond.

The last thing she saw before the darkness took her was the massive, looming silhouette of the beast standing over her, its breath heavy and slow.

Then, everything faded to black.

———

Emily screamed, her voice raw with desperation, her throat aching from the force of it.

John's voice joined hers, hoarse and frantic, echoing against the cavern walls. They didn't know who was out there—if it was a rescuer, an enemy, or something worse—but they couldn't afford to stay silent.

She had nearly lost all hope when she heard it.

A voice—familiar, urgent.

"Emily!"

Her breath hitched in her throat, her heart pounding. Evan.

She craned her neck, searching for him, and finally saw his figure silhouetted against the faint light filtering through the cave. He stood at the edge of the pit, staring down, eyes scanning wildly.

Relief crashed over her like a tidal wave. She choked on a sob, tears spilling freely down her dirty face.

"Evan!" she cried.

His eyes locked onto hers. "Hold on, I'm getting you out of there."

John slumped against the rock beside her, his chest rising and falling in rapid, shallow breaths. He was in shock, his body trembling from both exhaustion and disbelief.

Evan looked around, searching for anything that could help, but the pit was deep—just out of reach. He let out a frustrated curse, then ripped off his jacket, extending it down as far as he could.

"Grab on!" he shouted.

Emily forced her aching limbs to move, her body screaming in protest as she reached up. She grasped onto the jacket's sleeve with both hands, and with a painful, gritted effort, Evan pulled her upward.

She clawed her way over the edge, collapsing onto solid ground, gasping for air.

Evan barely had time to acknowledge her relief before turning back to John.

"Come on, Hadley!" he urged, extending the jacket again.

John hesitated for a moment, staring up at Evan with hollow eyes, still lost in his own unraveling thoughts.

"Dad!" Emily called, desperation seeping into her tone. "Move!"

Something in her voice shook John out of his daze. Gritting his teeth, he forced himself to climb, his movements sluggish and pained. Evan pulled, using every ounce of his strength to haul the older man up. John tumbled onto solid ground, groaning in agony.

They barely had a second to breathe before a deep *thud* echoed through the cave.

Emily's blood ran cold.

The ground beneath them vibrated slightly, the rhythmic sound growing closer.

The creature was coming back.

Evan reacted instantly. "Get behind me!"

Emily and John stumbled back, pressing against the cavern wall as Evan raised his rifle. His hands were steady, his breath controlled, his finger pressing lightly against the trigger.

The creature's heavy footfalls grew louder, its massive form looming at the end of the tunnel.

Evan inhaled. Squeeze the trigger—

Before he could fire, a deafening volley of gunfire erupted behind the creature.

The cave filled with blinding flashes, the rapid *pop-pop-pop* of automatic weapons echoing through the stone walls. The beast let out a screeching wail, stumbling forward, its massive body twisting as bullets ripped through it.

Emily, Evan, and John dropped to the ground, shielding themselves from the onslaught. The creature roared, flailing as the gunfire intensified. It tried to charge, but the barrage was relentless, its strength failing.

Then, with one final tortured howl, it collapsed, its massive body slamming onto the rocky ground with a sickening *thud.*

Silence fell over the cave.

Evan slowly lifted his head, blinking through the haze of smoke and dust. Bright beams of light cut through the cavern.

Then came the voices.

"Move in!"

"Clear the area!"

The sound of boots stomping across stone.

Emily squinted as figures in camouflage emerged from the darkness, their weapons raised, their movements precise. They weren't police.

They were military.

A soldier with a Special Forces insignia approached, his expression unreadable beneath his tactical helmet. He scanned them with sharp, assessing eyes before speaking.

"You injured?"

Emily swallowed hard, nodding weakly.

"Anyone else in here?" the soldier asked.

"No," Evan managed, his voice hoarse. "We were the last."

The soldier nodded, then motioned for them to move. "Come with us."

Emily stumbled to her feet, her legs weak, her body aching with every step. As they passed the creature's massive corpse, John slowed, staring down at it. His face was unreadable, his body trembling as he reached out.

He placed his hand over the creature's.

A bizarre, misplaced moment of respect.

Before anyone could say anything, another figure approached—a man with an air of authority, wearing a camouflage uniform with a distinct insignia. He had a square jaw, cold eyes, and the hardened demeanor of a seasoned soldier.

The Colonel.

He didn't waste time. "Dr. Hadley?"

John turned slowly, his expression dazed. "Yes."

The Colonel's gaze flicked to the dead creature, then back to John. "Come with us."

John hesitated but ultimately obeyed, allowing himself to be led away.

Emily moved to follow, but Evan grabbed her hand.

She turned to him, her breath unsteady.

They stepped outside the cave to a scene of organized chaos.

Helicopters hovered above, their blades chopping through the air. Soldiers were everywhere, moving with practiced efficiency, speaking in clipped, controlled tones. Large vehicles had been stationed along the ridge, their headlights illuminating the rugged landscape.

Then Emily's eyes caught on something.

A group of soldiers standing near a black body bag.

Torres.

Evan stiffened, his hand tightening in Emily's. He turned, his jaw clenched as Sheriff Carter approached. His expression was grim, his usual bravado stripped away.

"Torres?" Evan asked, though he already knew the answer.

Carter exhaled through his nose, looking away briefly before nodding.

"She didn't make it."

Evan ran a hand down his face, his shoulders slumping.

Carter sighed, rubbing his temple. "And Reynolds?"

Evan shook his head. "Neither did he."

Carter's expression darkened, the loss weighing on him heavily. He looked over the chaos unfolding around them, the military presence, the helicopters, the urgency of the operation.

Evan followed his gaze. "What the hell is all this?"

Carter let out a sharp breath, keeping his voice low. "After you left, I was... *visited*. They told me they were taking over. I don't know who they are, and I don't know how they knew." He gestured toward the soldiers. "But now they're running the show."

Evan glanced toward the Colonel, who was now speaking with John a few yards away. "What do they want with Hadley?"

Carter shook his head. "No idea. But I'd bet my badge they don't want anyone talking about this."

Carter studied Evan and Emily carefully.

"What did you see in there?"

Evan hesitated.

Emily's fingers tightened around his.

He turned to Carter, his expression unreadable.

"Nothing," he said.

Emily nodded. "Same."

Carter let out a long breath, then gave a small, knowing nod.

"Probably for the best."

Evan pulled Emily closer, walking her toward the

waiting medics as the sounds of military activity buzzed around them.

There would be questions. There would be investigations.

But some things?

Some things were best left buried.

CHAPTER 8

The hospital room was quiet except for the steady beep of the heart monitor and the occasional murmur of voices from the hallway. The sterile white walls and the scent of disinfectant made the place feel colder than it already was, but Emily didn't care. She was alive. That was all that mattered.

She shifted slightly in the hospital bed, wincing as the bruises along her ribs protested. Evan sat in the chair beside her, arms crossed, his expression unreadable. They had barely spoken since the previous night—there wasn't much to say.

Then came a sharp knock at the door.

Evan immediately straightened, his hand resting on his thigh as if instinctively preparing for something worse.

The door swung open, and two men stepped inside.

One of them was a young officer in a crisp, dark uniform, holding a clipboard and pen. His eyes were sharp and calculating, but it was the man beside him who made Emily's stomach tighten.

The Colonel.

He looked the same as he had in the cave—broad-shouldered, stone-faced, his uniform immaculate. His cold, measured gaze landed on Emily first, then Evan.

"Good morning, Miss Hadley. Deputy Morgan," he said, his voice even, controlled. "How are you feeling?"

Emily exchanged a glance with Evan, then looked back at the Colonel. "I've been better."

The Colonel gave a short nod. "Understandable." He gestured to the junior officer. "We need to debrief you both about the events in the cave. I trust you'll cooperate."

Evan exhaled sharply through his nose but didn't argue. Emily sat up a little, wincing as she adjusted her pillow.

"Fine," she said. "Ask your questions."

The debriefing was methodical. The Colonel asked, and they answered.

How did you enter the cave?

How long were you inside?

What did you see?

When did you first encounter the entity?

How did it behave?

The junior officer scribbled down every detail, his pen scratching against the paper with efficiency.

Neither Emily nor Evan bothered to hold back—there was no point. They recounted everything, from the moment they found the cave entrance to the horror inside. They told them about Jake's fate, about Reynolds and Torres, about the creature's terrifying speed and strength.

When they finished, the Colonel folded his hands behind his back, exchanging a glance with his subordinate. The younger man reached into his folder and pulled out two identical documents, placing them on the hospital tray in front of Emily and Evan.

Emily picked hers up, skimming the bolded title at the top:

NON-DISCLOSURE AGREEMENT

She looked up at the Colonel, her stomach tightening. "You're serious?"

The Colonel's face remained unreadable. "You sign, and this never happened."

Evan frowned, looking at the document in his hands. "And if we don't sign?"

The junior officer adjusted his glasses and spoke for the first time, his voice flat. "Then you come with us."

Silence.

Emily and Evan exchanged a glance. It wasn't a choice. Not really.

Emily swallowed hard, grabbed the pen, and signed.

Evan hesitated, jaw clenching, then sighed and did the same.

The junior officer collected both documents, sliding them back into his folder.

The Colonel took a step closer, looking between them with an air of finality. His voice was calm, but there was an unmistakable edge beneath it.

"You will never speak of this again," he said. "Not to your families. Not to your friends. Not to anyone. Am I clear?"

Emily nodded.

Evan gave a slow, measured nod.

The Colonel studied them for a moment longer, then turned toward the door. As he reached for the handle,

Emily couldn't help herself.

"What about my father?" she asked, her voice firm.

The Colonel paused, glancing back over his shoulder.

"He's coming with us," he said. "To help."

Emily's stomach twisted. "Help with what, the creature?"

The Colonel gave the smallest of smirks, the first hint of emotion she had seen on his face.

"What creature?" he said smoothly. "But I can tell you this. You'll hear from him soon and again, no discussing anything."

Then he turned and left, the junior officer following close behind.

Emily and Evan sat in silence, listening to the sound of their boots echoing down the hall.

Finally, Evan leaned back in his chair, exhaling sharply. He ran a hand through his hair, shaking his head. "Well. That was fun."

Emily huffed out a tired laugh.

He turned to look at her, expression softening. "You okay?"

Emily hesitated, then shook her head. "No."

Evan nodded. "Yeah. Me neither."

The room fell into silence again. The weight of everything hung heavy in the air.

Evan finally broke it. "So…" he started, tilting his head toward the hospital tray. "Can we talk about anything else besides what happened?"

Emily blinked, then let out a quiet, almost breathless laugh.

"Yes," she said. "Please."

Evan smirked. "Alright. So this hospital food sucks. What can I go get you?"

Emily smiled, sinking back into the pillow.

"Pizza," she said. "Pepperoni. Please."

Evan stood, stretching slightly. "You got it."

And for the first time in what felt like forever, Emily let herself breathe.

EPILOGUE

John Hadley peered out the small helicopter window, the desert landscape stretching endlessly beneath him. The rolling dunes, barren plateaus, and empty, sun-scorched terrain looked almost alien.

It was the first time he had seen open sky since being dragged into that cave. And now, here he was, flying toward something even more unimaginable.

In the back of the helicopter, sealed in a heavy-duty freezer box, was the creature. His creature.

John exhaled slowly, steadying himself. *Finally.* Finally, he had proof. He had dedicated his entire life to being ridiculed, mocked, dismissed as a fringe scientist. But he had been right. And now, he would have the opportunity to study what no one else had before.

I knew they knew, he thought. *I just knew it.*

The helicopter began to descend, its shadow stretching across the cracked desert floor. A sprawling facility came into view—rows of hangars, a cluster of nondescript buildings, and a massive runway cutting through the sand.

They landed on the tarmac, and the second the rotor blades slowed, the side door opened. The dry heat slammed into him immediately, a stark contrast to the cold air-conditioned interior of the chopper.

Standing just outside, waiting, was the Colonel.

John stepped out onto the scorching pavement, shielding his eyes against the sun. The Colonel gave him a curt nod.

"Welcome to Groom Lake."

John's brows furrowed. "And where exactly is Groom Lake?"

The Colonel smirked slightly. "You're in Nevada, Mr. Hadley, or should I say, Dr. Hadley. Now, please come with me."

"But I'm no longer a doctor, I lost that designation a few years back when the university..."

The Colonel stopped and said, "None of that matters now, here you'll be given the respect you deserve, here you're Dr. Hadley."

"Ah, wow, great, thank you." John glanced back at the helicopter, where soldiers were carefully unloading the freezer box containing the creature. "What about it?"

"Don't worry," the Colonel assured him. "It's going somewhere safe. Soon, you'll be examining it yourself."

A Jeep was waiting for them. Without another word, John climbed in alongside the Colonel, who started the vehicle and drove across the tarmac. The heat shimmered off the pavement, distorting the surrounding desert like a mirage.

Up ahead, a massive hangar loomed—but as they

approached, John noticed something different about it. It wasn't just a typical aircraft hangar.

It was carved into the side of the mountain itself.

They drove inside, the temperature dropping instantly as the massive metal doors sealed behind them.

The hangar was empty. No planes. No vehicles. Just a few stray personnel moving with quiet efficiency.

The Colonel pulled the Jeep to a stop and motioned for John to follow. They walked deeper into the facility, stopping at a briefing room with a steel table and two chairs.

A familiar figure was already waiting inside.

The junior officer from the hospital.

He carried the same clipboard, the same precise demeanor. He gave John a nod, then handed him a stack of documents.

"Please read through and sign," the officer said flatly.

John flipped through the papers, skimming them. "What is this?"

"It assures you understand that you are now working at a top-secret facility. Your work here is classified. You are not to discuss anything you see, hear, or learn while at Groom Lake."

John glanced up. "And Emily?"

"She's fine," the Colonel assured him. "You'll see her again. But for now, you'll be working and living here."

John's fingers tightened on the papers, his mind whirling. But deep down, he knew there was no turning back.

He signed.

The Colonel collected the forms and gave him a satisfied

nod. "You were lucky, Dr. Hadley. That thing in the cave could have torn you apart."

John scoffed. "It tried."

The Colonel smirked and motioned for him to follow.

They walked down a long, stark white hallway, the walls pristine and sterile. At the end of the hall, they entered a lab—gleaming steel tables, bright overhead lights, and an array of medical equipment.

John's heart pounded as they stepped into a smaller room at the back.

It looked like a morgue.

Several refrigerated storage units lined the walls, similar to those used for cadavers. A single examination table sat in the center, its lights casting a sterile glow.

John swallowed. "Is *it* in one of these?"

The Colonel nodded. "Yes. But so are the others."

John turned sharply. "What others?"

The Colonel's expression remained neutral. "There are other cryptids we'd like you to examine." He checked his watch. "Dr. Casey will assist you. He'll answer your questions from here. Let me know if you need anything."

Without another word, the Colonel exited the room, the heavy doors sealing behind him.

For a long moment, John stood alone, staring at the refrigerators lining the walls.

His curiosity overpowered his nerves.

Slowly, he walked to the nearest one and pulled open the sliding tray.

A body was revealed.

It looked similar to a Bigfoot, but its fur was white.

John's breath caught in his throat.

An alpine variety? A different species? A mutation? A Yeti?
Shaking, he slid the tray back in and moved to the next.

He hesitated. Then he pulled it open.

What he saw wasn't a Bigfoot.

It was something else entirely.

It had the features of a wolf—long snout, pointed ears, thick fur—but its body was humanoid.

John's hands trembled as he exhaled.

A Dogman.

He had heard of these before—stories whispered in cryptid circles, legends that had no scientific foundation.

But this wasn't a legend.

This was *real*.

The door behind him suddenly opened, and a man in a white lab coat stepped in.

Dr. Casey.

"You must be Dr. John Hadley," the doctor said, offering a small smile.

John nodded, still staring at the creature on the table. "Are all these full?"

Dr. Casey chuckled. "You bet. And this doesn't even count the overflow."

John's eyes snapped to him. "Overflow?"

Dr. Casey motioned for him to follow.

They exited the small morgue-like room and walked down another hallway until they reached a massive steel door.

Dr. Casey swiped his badge, and the door hissed open.

The lights flickered on, revealing a colossal storage room.

John froze.

Dozens of refrigeration units lined the walls—stretching far beyond what he could count.

"These too?" he whispered.

Dr. Casey nodded, smirking. "Yep."

John's mind spun. "What else is in here?"

Dr. Casey's grin widened. "Oh, some aren't even from this world."

He gestured toward a specific unit. "Go ahead. Open that one."

John hesitated. Then he stepped forward, grasped the handle, and pulled.

Lying on the tray was a Gray alien.

Its thin, elongated limbs. Its smooth, pale skin. Its large, black, lifeless eyes staring upward.

John felt his throat tighten.

"…Is that a…?"

Dr. Casey nodded. "Yep."

John ran a hand down his face. "So we're *not* alone."

Dr. Casey smirked. "Wait until you see what else we have. But not right now. First, let's get to work on your Bigfoot. Maybe at break, I'll show you the rest."

John exhaled slowly, his hands still shaking.

Dr. Casey clapped him on the back.

"Welcome to S4-Biologicals Division, Dr. Hadley."

The End

Grab the other volumes in the series.

Cryptid Chronicles: Wendigo Winter
Cryptid Chronicles: Night Stalker
Cryptid Chronicles: The Beast
Cryptid Chronicles: The Cave
Cryptid Chronicles: The Hunt

ABOUT THE AUTHOR

Ethan Hayes grew up in Oklahoma and moved to Texas when he attended Texas A&M. Upon graduation he was hired by Texas Parks and Wildlife and remained there until he retired twenty-two years later. He currently lives in southeast Texas with his wife and two dogs. When he's not spending time enjoying the outdoors and writing, he sips a cold beer on his front porch while listening to Bluegrass music.

ALSO BY ETHAN HAYES

ALSO BY FREE REIGN PUBLISHING

STORIES FROM THE NICU

CRAZY MEDICAL STORIES

PAWSITIVE MOMENTS: LIFE IN A VETERINARY CLINIC

STORIES FROM THE NICU

VANISHED: STRANGE & MYSTERIOUS DISAPPEARANCES

DIAGNOSIS: RARE MEDICAL CASES

THE BIG BIGFOOT BOOK SERIES

THE MEGA MONSTER BOOK SERIES

LOST SOULS: 50 NATIONAL PARK DISAPPEARANCES

ON CALL: EMERGENCY ROOM STORIES

CURSED: TALES OF THE WORLD'S MOST HAUNTED OBJECTS

CRAZY AMBULANCE STORIES

IN YOUR OWN WORDS GUIDED JOURNAL SERIES

TODAY I'M GRATEFUL FOR…DAILY JOURNAL

ONE YEAR / ONE QUESTION: DAILY JOURNAL

Printed in Dunstable, United Kingdom

77896892R00088